Piano Man

J.L. Fredrick

Lovstad Publishing
Poynette, Wisconsin
www.Lovstadpublishing.com

PIANO MAN

First Edition

ISBN: 0692229094
ISBN-13: 978-0692229095

Printed in the United States of America

Cover design by Lovstad Publishing

For Roger and Beverly, Michael and Kris

OTHER BOOKS BY J.L. FREDRICK

Across the Dead Line
Across the Second Dead Line
The Private Journal of Clancy Crane
Unfinished Business
The Other End of the Tunnel
Another Shade of Gray
The Gaslight Knights
Thunder in the Night
The Great Train Robbery of Monroe County
Mad City Bust
September Ten
Aftermath
Cursed by the Wind
Dance With a Tornado

NON-FICTION

Rivers, Roads, and Rails
Ghostville

Piano Man

ONE

"We could use a good piano man."

Clay looked at Christian with utmost seriousness. "And where do y'all think we'll find one here?"

"We could go into the city and find one."

The thought of venturing out to Baraboo was secretly intriguing to both, but rather than jumping up in jubilation to begin their journey, they sat quietly at their table and sipped the dark ale. Simon had been gone all day—again—and the boys were eager to get back to work. Work to them, of course, was performing on a stage, and soon there would be plenty of people to enjoy their performances. All winter they had practiced their skits and songs that had been successful back in Silver Spring at Tanglewood after the theater closed, and they had even tried them out on small groups here in the *Cliff House*. But if they were to perform before larger audiences at the *Cha-*

teau, they needed a piano player to appear more professional. So far, their efforts to find one had rendered nothing.

"Did I hear you say you need a piano player?"

Christian and Clay spun around to face the voice that had just spoken to them.

"I couldn't help but overhear..."

The boys at the table stared at the tall, dark-haired fellow standing there. None of them spoke for a while, just trying to size each other up.

"Do you play the piano?" Christian finally asked. It didn't seem likely; the fellow didn't look the type.

"No," the lad replied. "But I have a friend..."

Clay kicked the chair next to him out away from the table. "Have a seat," he said.

As the fellow sat, pulling the chair closer, Clay half stood and offered his right hand. "My name is Clay Edwards... and this is Christian Parker."

"My name is Roscoe Connor. Pleased to meet you both." He shook their hands and then eyed Clay. "I saw you playin' cards last night at the hotel. You sure 'nough cleaned everybody out."

Christian leaned in. "Best not sit down with this guy at the poker table. He doesn't lose."

"What he means to say," Clay corrected, "is that I *usually* win more than I lose."

"Yes, I saw evidence of that last night," said Roscoe.

"So, who's your piano-playin' friend?" Christian asked, looking around. "Where is he?"

"Oh, he's not here. His name's Marty Mason.

He's in Baraboo."

"Where can we find him?"

"That's hard to say."

"Well... could you take us to him?"

Roscoe stared at Christian for a moment with reluctance in his eyes. "I'm here for a week of fishing.
After that?"

"I'll pay your train fare if you'll go with us tomorrow."

"I don't know..."

"Aw, c'mon, Roscoe," Clay pleaded. "How long
can it take? A couple hours there and back?"

"I'll have to think about it."

"The first train to Baraboo is at eight o'clock in
the morning," Christian said. "We could be back here
by ten."

"And you'll hardly miss any fishing time at all,"
Clay added.

"Well, I suppose..."

"Great!" Christian said. "We'll meet you at the
depot at seven-forty-five."

Clay Edwards had been eagerly waiting for spring
since the very first November snowfall. His peculiar
little drawl that stamped him as Southern born made
it quite clear he was never conditioned for Wisconsin
winters. Content to stay by a warm fire, he'd managed to find a few poker games to keep him occupied
during the cold months. Many a visitor from the big
cities went back home with lighter pockets after an
evening or two at the game table across from Clay.

Here, though, the stakes weren't always as high as in the gold and silver boomtowns of the West, but Clay didn't really care; it was simply a good way to pass the time, and to keep spending money in his pocket.

Christian Parker, though, was accustomed to winter; he'd grown up in Denver. Winter was just a normal part of the year to him; he had skated on the frozen lake and had enjoyed the horse-drawn sleigh rides, although he, too, vigorously welcomed the springtime.

Nearly nine months had passed since they left Montana and arrived at Devil's Lake Village. They had endured the bitter Wisconsin winter, but now the ice was gone from the lake; warm spring air gave promise to the forthcoming summer. Nothing seemed grander than the verdant luster creeping onto the forested hills, for the dreary chill of winter and its blustery wind, the messenger of frosty and snow-filled days had erased the memory of crimson and gold and fiery orange that had painted those glorious October hills. Devil's Lake stretched and yawned as it awoke from its long, icy sleep, welcoming the warmth of the April sun and clamor of ducks and geese upon its placid waters. Soon it would host bathers and rowers and anglers, as the lake and its hotels and campsites had become a most popular resort destination to people from far and near. The *Chicago and Northwestern* railway trains would deposit vacationers from the big cities like Chicago, Milwaukee, and St. Paul by the hundreds and thousands all summer long, and Devil's Lake Village would be a very busy place.

Simon Bordeaux, the man responsible for them being there at Devil's Lake, had envisioned something grand. In the recent past, his endeavors in the theater business had all been relatively short-lived, moving from one mining camp to another, satisfying the entertainment needs and desires for communities that were destined to ghostdom when the mines played out. But nearby Baraboo was different; it was a show town, home of the Ringling Brothers Circus. One thing was certain: unlike the boomtowns in the West, Baraboo was a well-established city that would be there for a long time. It held a population quite ample to support a theater for the performing arts, and it would only be a matter of time until Simon had one established.

When Simon, Christian, and Clay boarded the train in Silver Spring, Montana nine months ago, they were parting with good friends; they were leaving behind a magnificent opera house. But they were also saying goodbye to a town that was destined for destruction. The mines had played out and the majority of the population had moved on, abandoning homes and deserting businesses. Within a few short months, a madman gunned down the proprietor of the only operating hotel left, and then set fire to the rest of the town, leaving nothing but ashes and charred memories.

That winter, Christian received a telegram from his good friend Clancy Crane who, by then, was working aboard a riverboat on the Lower Mississippi River.

They exchanged many letters after that, in which Clancy told of the devastating events that had destroyed Silver Spring and his harrowing experiences of survival. After the smoke cleared, warding off looters and outlaws in order to protect his dead brother's hotel, the only remaining building—Tanglewood Lodge—had not been easy, and finally, it seemed best to just leave. *"There was nothing to stay for,"* Clancy wrote. *"Somehow, I knew nobody was ever coming back. I bid farewell to my sister-in-law and my niece in Wellington, and hopped on a south bound steamer working as a deck hand. Three weeks later our boat was in St. Louis, and two weeks after that we arrived at New Orleans. We will stay on the Lower Mississippi all winter."* Of all the friends they had left behind, they missed Clancy most. His brother's hotel had been home for them after the opera house closed, so they had spent much time together. But their combined efforts and coaxing couldn't get Clancy to accompany them to Wisconsin.

Young as they were—Christian barely nineteen, and Clay, twenty, although his boyish looks made him seem much younger—they were seasoned stage performers. Christian's angelic singing voice melted half the ladies' hearts, and Clay's delightful Southern acting charm liquefied the other half. There could be little doubt why Simon Bordeaux, the troupe manager and producer, had lured them to Wisconsin with him; audiences loved these two adorable personalities, and rarely failed to fill the house when they performed. But those audiences had been in the wild

8

Western mining camps; this was Wisconsin, where audiences had already been exposed to sophisticated stage arts for quite some time. Simon, though, was still optimistic that his two star performers could capture hearts in the Midwest just as well as in the Western theater. He was counting on it.

And there could be little doubt that they were getting restless, eager to be performing again.

As the train slowly pulled away from the Devil's Lake station the next morning and rolled along the edge of the lake, Roscoe Connor gazed out over the water, yearning to be there with a fishing pole in his hands. His father, a merchant in Baraboo, had finally relented, and given him a week to spend at the lake before the busy tourist season began, when the place would be overrun by big city dwellers. And now he was giving up precious time he had been longing for all winter, to find his friend Marty Mason, just because Marty could play the piano.

"Don't look so sad," Clay said. He stretched his arm behind Roscoe's neck and playfully patted his shoulder. "You'll be back out there fishing in no time."

"That is," Roscoe replied. "If we can find Marty right away."

"Why should he be so hard to find?"

"Mason could be anywhere. Until the Ringling Brothers come back for the season..."

"Ringling Brothers? They're the circus people?"

"Yeah... one of the most popular circuses in the

9

country. Marty worked for them all last summer, and he says he's gonna work for them again this year, too."

"What does he do in the circus?"

"He's a musician. He traveled with them last summer."

"Hallelujah! Did y'all hear that, Christian? Our new piano player traveled with the circus! Just like Fingers Malone."

"He's not *our* piano player yet," Christian returned. "And if he already has a job with the circus, we might be wasting our time." He turned to Roscoe. "Why didn't you tell us that before we started on a wild goose chase?"

"You didn't ask," Roscoe replied. "Why do you need a piano player anyway?"

"We're performers of a theater troupe. We came here from Montana, but we came *without* a piano player."

"Montana!" Roscoe said.

"Yes," Christian explained. "We had a very successful theater in a mining town, but when the mine was finished, so were we. All the people of the town moved on..." Then, with a bit of melancholy in his voice he added, "And our opera house, the grand Crystal Palace died."

"So Simon went scoutin' for a new place," Clay added. "And we ended up here."

"Who's Simon?" Roscoe asked.

"Simon Bordeaux is our director. He owned the Crystal Palace... and he kinda runs the whole show.

But he couldn't talk Fingers into coming with us."

"Who's Fingers?"

"He was the piano player at the hotel where we lived," Christian said. "When our theater closed, Clay and I kept performing at the hotel now and then, and Fingers provided the music."

"So, what happened to your theater musicians?" Roscoe asked.

"Most of them joined up with other troupes, but Simon thinks some of them... and some of the actors, too... will rejoin us here. He's been sending a lot of telegrams and letters."

By then, the train was rumbling along at speed through the countryside. Baraboo was not far; in ten minutes they would arrive at the station, and their search for the pianist would begin.

TWO

"**I** reckon we can start lookin' at his house," Roscoe suggested when they had disembarked the train.

It did seem a logical place to begin, however, Marty was not there, nor did his mother have a clue where he had spent the night. "I thought," she said, "That some of the circus people had returned, and he was with them."

But the circus people had not returned yet; their summer quarters were empty and quiet.

"So where to now?" asked Clay.

"We'll just have to walk around town... try to spot him somewhere."

"So *you* can spot him," Christian said. "Clay and I don't know who we're looking for."

"He's about my size," Roscoe explained. "Maybe a little taller."

"Well... that narrows it right down. What color is his hair?"

"Like sand. But it's cut short, and his cap covers

13

most of it."

"What color is his cap?"

"Like sand."

"Now we're getting somewhere."

"Marty's got freckles," Roscoe offered.

"Okay! Okay!" said Clay. "We'll just follow y'all."

They toured the town, all except one street that Roscoe explained he had to avoid. "My father's store is on that street, and if he sees me here in town, he'll make me come back to work. I'm *supposed* to be out at the lake fishin', y' know."

The whistles of the next train to the lake had been heard long ago, still with no sign of the piano player. But a few of Roscoe's acquaintances had seen Marty that morning; he couldn't be far away.

By noon they had nearly given up all hope of finding Marty when Roscoe stopped in his tracks to take another look down an alley. "There he is," he said, pointing to a group of rough-looking characters. "Marty's the one in the yellow shirt."

Clay and Christian were glad to have finally ended the hunt; but the gathering in the alley didn't look like a friendly one. The yellow-shirted fellow was certainly outnumbered by five slovenly-attired ruffians; it appeared as if Marty Mason was about to become the recipient of some brutal treatment.

"HEY! MASON!" Roscoe called out.

That drew the attention of the gang from Marty just long enough for him to slip away, around the corner from his attackers. By the time they realized he was gone, Clay, Christian and Roscoe had taken advantage of their confused state to make an exit as well. They dashed down the street and ducked into the next alley. On a dead run, Christian and Clay followed Roscoe; he knew his way around the town, and they sincerely hoped he would lead them to an effective escape.

After two more blocks they stopped and listened at the corner, trying to detect any approach by the gang. They heard running footsteps, but it was only one pair of feet. Clay boldly stepped out to look. A bright yellow shirt was coming right at him at full speed. He reached out to grab the runner, spun him around and pulled him into the alley.

The fellow in the yellow shirt was taken by such alarm that he was winding up for a good fist fight before he realized that his friend, Roscoe was there.

"Go ahead!" he said to Clay. "Take your best shot!" Both his fists were clenched, drawn back, ready to strike. But then, as he eyed Clay dressed in a fancy black three-piece suit and bowler, standing before him with no intensions of engaging in battle, he relaxed a little, but still poised for defense if it became necessary.

"Take it easy, Mason," Roscoe said.

Marty Mason reluctantly turned to the familiar voice. "Connor! What are you doing here?" he asked his friend, still ready for a skirmish.

"Relax, Mason. They're friends."

Marty stared at Clay, and then at Christian. "How do I know I can trust 'em?"

"You'll just have to take my word," Roscoe replied

as he gripped Marty's forearm.

They could hear the angry growls and shouts of Marty's enemies about a block away. There was little time to discuss the merits of friendship; escape for Marty from these thugs was top priority.

"I have a plan," Clay informed the others. He hastily inspected Marty and Roscoe, comparing their size. "You two... trade shirts and caps."

The two friends stared at Clay, puzzled. "What—"

"Don't argue," Clay insisted. "Just DO IT! QUICK-LY!"

Marty and Roscoe seemed to realize that Clay might have a good plan in mind. They swiftly followed the instructions, exchanging the clothing. The malicious voices were coming nearer.

"Now," Clay said. "Marty? Do y'all have any objections to taking a little train ride with us?"

Marty peered up the alley where the gang would appear any second, and then back at Clay. "Train ride?"

"No time for questions," Clay said. "It's that or we can leave y'all here to face those *friends* of yours on your own."

"Okay..." Marty answered. "I'll go with you."

"Christian," Clay said. "Take Marty down this alley and then go to the train station. Roscoe and I will stay here long enough to draw their attention with this yellow shirt. It should give y'all enough time to reach the station... they won't know where you went."

"And what about you?" Marty asked.

"Don't worry about us. I'll think of something. Now, GO! We'll catch up with y'all at the station."

Christian and Marty, now clad in Roscoe's faded blue shirt and dark blue cap, rushed down the alley and around the corner. Clay instructed Roscoe to turn his back to the other end of the alley where the gang was just entering.

"THERE HE IS!" the gang leader yelled. "LET'S GET HIM!"

Clay sensed Roscoe's fright as they listened to the hurried footsteps coming toward them. "Don't be afraid," he told Roscoe. "Simply turn around nice and easy when I give you a nod."

Clay counted five of them, all toting clubs of some sort; there was definitely murder in their eyes as they marched closer. The leader was a big fellow, at least six feet tall and rather stocky, built like a steamer trunk with legs and arms, clothes ragged, dirty and stained with sweat. The rest varied in size, but none were dressed any better than their chief, and all were determined to do harm to the fellow in the yellow shirt. They were about ten feet from Roscoe when Clay nodded. "Nice and easy," he reminded Roscoe in a low tone.

Roscoe slowly turned to face the assailants. "Hello, Jasper," he said. He tried to look unconcerned, but he knew he wasn't being very convincing. Even on this cool day, nervous sweat trickled down his back. Clay stepped beside him.

Upon seeing Roscoe's face, the gang leader stopped abruptly, holding his arms out to halt the others behind him. A jumble of shock, confusion, and disappointment washed over him as he stared at the target that had mysteriously changed. "Okay..." he said. "So... where's that rat?"

"To which rat would y'all be referring?" Clay said quite calmly.

Jasper still seemed baffled, and snarls kept coming from his followers. "Mason," the brute growled. "The one we followed here."

"Well," Clay replied. "There's no one else here... as y'all can plainly see."

Trying to make sense of the strange situation, Jasper looked Roscoe up and down, and then turned his focus on Clay, studying the fine clothes. Clay Edwards, in the prime of his life, just a little beyond twenty, not so tall but erect, continued to dress in the typical costume of the river gamblers—a dark, long-tailed coat, white shirt and black string tie, brocade vest, dark trousers, narrow at the bottom, and high-heeled boots polished like a mirror. He stood with supreme self-confidence without showing a hint of arrogance.

Jasper slapped the club he was holding into the palm of his free hand. Encountering a total stranger—especially one with the striking looks of Clay Edwards—was not what he had expected to find in that alley; he was stalling, trying to figure his next move, quite sure he had been hoodwinked but didn't know how. "Well, I think you must've helped him get away."

"Just why do y'all want to catch up with this *rat?*"

Clay asked. He was buying time as well.

"That's none of your business," Jasper snapped, and then it was quite clear that Jasper and his gang intended to make short work of the two standing between them and their intended victim.

Roscoe was familiar with the ruffians; they were the most feared bullies among the population of Baraboo. Those who *did* attend school—Jasper among them—passed their classes only because the teachers were afraid to fail them. As far as Roscoe was concerned, he had always stayed clear of them, and right now he would sooner be running away at full speed than to be standing there facing these thugs. At this point, his confidence was melting like ice cream under a July sun; neither he nor Clay were big enough to take on all five in an alley fight, particularly when the opposition was armed with clubs... and no doubt, some with knives. He wondered how Clay could stand there so calm in the face of imminent danger. Clay's good plan had turned sour, and now they were about to pay for their bravery.

As Jasper and a couple of his buddies stepped forward, muscles flexed for combat, Clay's right hand gave a sudden jerk. In the next instant, the aggressors were staring at the business end of his double-barreled .41 caliber Remington derringer that was always tucked in a pocket inside his coat sleeve, ready for any unexpected need of defense. Jasper and the other two abruptly stopped their advance, eyes as big as fried eggs in a pan fixed on the weapon. Even though it was small in size, its large caliber barrels appeared rather intimidating.

"Y-you c-can't h-hit the b-broad side of a b-barn with that little pea-shooter," Jasper stuttered nervously.

"On the contrary," Clay said. "At this range I *don't* miss."

"B-but you only have two shots," Jasper said. "And there's five of us."

"Maybe," replied Clay. "But the first one will find *you*, Jasper, and then your friend beside you." He held out his left hand, palm up, revealing two more cartridges. "And I can reload before the two of you hit the ground. Believe me... I've had plenty of practice."

The two roughnecks beside Jasper swiftly and meekly retreated to their comrades behind them.

Roscoe stared at the gun with surprise, too, and then his eyes raced back and forth from Jasper to Clay. Although he had suddenly regained a little confidence, his instincts governed a couple cautious steps in retreat. Jasper, although stunned by the sight of the firepower, wasn't backing down.

Clay remained steadfast with his stiff right arm outstretched, the derringer pointed at Jasper's chest. "Now," he said calmly. "Maybe you boys should reconsider your desire for rat hunting today. I'm sure y'all could find something more constructive to do." His poker face never flinched or displayed any sign of emotion. His unblinking eyes were welded to Jasper's.

There was a chance, Jasper thought, that this

Southern silver-tongued dandy was bluffing. But there was also the chance that he wasn't. He didn't look like a killer, but he acted much too calm for any man in his position. "Y-you won't pull that trigger," Jasper taunted nervously, stepping closer.

Clay pulled back the hammer and it sounded its distinct, unmistakable click that echoed between the buildings. "Take one more step in this direction, Mr. Jasper, and your pals will be carryin' y'all out of this alley."

"Y-you're bluffing."

"I've shot men before under much less threatening circumstances," Clay said in his soft, calm Southern drawl. "Y'all are comin' at me with a deadly weapon. I don't take kindly to getting beat over the head with a lead pipe."

Jasper's four disciple dogs were backing away. "Come on, Jasper," one pleaded with him.

"This ain't worth gettin' shot," another called out.

"I don't think he's bluffing, Jasper!" another cried.

"Let's get outa here 'fore this lunatic shoots us all," the fourth one urged.

Their voices were shallow and scared. Jasper listened to their petitions, and without admitting his own fear, he took a step back and dropped the pipe to his side. He now had his excuse to retreat: "Okay, you donkey spit," he snarled. "I guess the boys aren't wantin' t' fight today... so I guess I'll stick with them." He took several steps backward to rejoin the gang, and then they all started back stepping rapidly out of the alley. Half-way, they turned to walk forward, but still glancing over their shoulders to see Clay still standing in the same position with outstretched arm and derringer pointing their way.

Clay remained in that posture until the last one disappeared around the corner. He took a deep breath, dropped his arm, relaxed, and turned to where Roscoe stood six feet behind him. A little shaken by the incident and still quite tense, Roscoe stared in disbelief. No one had ever stood up to Jasper Blackburn and his bunch without receiving at least a black eye, multiple bruises and a knot on the head, if not worse.

Clay deposited the Remington back in its sleeve pocket, completely out of sight. "We have to get to the train station," he said. "What's the shortest way?"

Roscoe pointed his thumb over his shoulder, the opposite end of the alley from where Jasper left. It wasn't necessarily the *shortest* route to the depot, but he didn't want another confrontation. Clay gripped his arm, spun him around and started walking briskly toward the street. "Lead the way to the station," he told Roscoe.

THREE

C hristian held four tickets to Devil's Lake. He breathed a little easier when he spotted Clay and Roscoe entering the crowded, busy station house. Marty Mason had hunkered down in a chair back in a corner, trying to stay out of sight. Neither of them was aware of Clay and Roscoe's narrow escape, nor of the gang's close proximity to the station. Clay had seen them, and he was quite certain that Jasper had followed them, perhaps seeking revenge.

"We have to get on that train... NOW!" Clay informed the others. He pushed Christian and Roscoe toward the platform door, and then grabbed Marty's arm and hoisted him up from the chair, practically dragging him to the boarding platform.

Roscoe spoke up: "But this train—"

"No time to be choosy," Clay interrupted calmly and continued to urge the others to a coach door. Once in the coach, Clay instructed the others to sit in seats away from the windows. Christian knew Clay's background well enough to know that he was a master at hasty get-away, and he also knew that Clay must have good reason for this one.

They heard the "All aboard" call by the conductor, and a few seconds later the shrill cry of the whistle. The train jolted forward, rumbling slowly away from the station. Clay saw Jasper and his gang through the windows, but it didn't appear they had any clue that the foursome was on the train. They seemed to still be searching among the people on the platform.

A few minutes later the conductor came by asking for tickets. Christian handed them over to be punched.

"How far are you boys going?" the conductor asked curiously.

"To Devil's Lake."

The conductor laughed. "You're on the wrong train "We're headed to North Freedom and Rock Springs."

"Where's North Freedom?"

"The opposite direction from the lake."

Roscoe joined the conversation. "I tried to tell you back at the station."

"Well," Clay said. "We'll just have to buy more tickets to North Freedom."

"Tell you what," the conductor said. "I'll just let you boys get off at North Freedom. Next train back to the lake will be along in about two hours."

The station at North Freedom wasn't so crowded. A few other passengers had gotten off there, but most of them were already gone. The foursome stood on the platform watching the westbound train disappear around the bend.

"What are we gonna do here for two hours?" Christian asked no one in particular.

"One thing you *could* do," Marty said, "Is to explain what I'm doing here with a couple of people I don't know. You practically kidnapped me, y' know."

"I'd call it more like savin' your ass from getting beaten to a pulp!" said Clay. After a dramatic pause he added: "A little appreciation?"

Marty thought for a moment; he hadn't said much the whole time since the miraculous rescue by these strangers. Christian had introduced himself at the Baraboo station, but Marty had responded only by speaking his name—no more. He realized that he had probably been somewhat rude and ungrateful for not thanking his saviors. "Thanks," he said in a meek tone, and then offered his right hand to Clay. "I don't know who you are, but I *am* grateful for what you did."

"I'm Clay Edwards, and I'm sure you already know Christian. Y'all prob'ly had a chance to get acquainted back at the last station."

"By name only," said Marty. He nodded to Christian. "I guess I wasn't too talkative back there."

Roscoe had remained silent, too, since the incident in the alley; Clay's behavior had extended far beyond what he expected, and so smoothly executed, there could be little doubt that experience in such matters had to exist. "Why do you carry a pistol?" he asked Clay in a tone that offered his suspicion of an outlaw.

"It's a derringer," Clay corrected. "Simply a means of protection associated with my former occupation."

"What are you talking about?" Marty broke in. "What pistol?"

"He pulled a gun—from where I don't know," Roscoe said. "That's how he got Jasper to back off."

Now Marty's curiosity rose to a new plateau; he had wondered why two finely dressed strangers had snatched him away from a hazardous state of affairs, potentially placing themselves in danger as well. They had no reason to jeopardize their own safety to help someone they did not know. "What kinda outlaws are you mixed up with, Roscoe?"

"Relax," Christian intervened. "We're not outlaws! It's true... Clay carries a derringer because he used to be a professional gambler."

"Gambler?" Marty sputtered.

"Yeah, that's probably so," said Roscoe. "I saw him playin' poker at the Cliff House... and he doesn't lose."

"Looks pretty young to be a professional gambler," Marty said.

"I started playin' poker when I was sixteen," Clay explained. "On a Mississippi riverboat where I worked. Thought I was just lucky at first, but then, one night I cleaned out a rich plantation owner of twenty-five thousand dollars. Decided right then and there that gambling was the best work for me."

"But you said... *used to be a gambler.*"

"I left the Mississippi—I'd had a few *bad experiences*—headed to the gold field boomtowns... that's when I eventually met Christian... after a few more hasty moves from one town to another."

"Bad experiences? Hasty moves?"

"It's unwritten law that when a man is accused of cheating... or he's challenged to a fight, he has the perfect right to promptly bring about his challenger's demise. But once that happens—and particularly if the man on the floor is a local—it's not a good idea to linger in that town too much longer."

Roscoe's and Marty's eyes widened like two little kids hearing a ghost story. "You mean... you... you..."

"Answered a few challenges?" Clay completed the question. "Yes... I did... but only when I was confronted with a deadly situation. Y'all must understand one thing: if a gambler backs down from a threat like that, one of two things happens... your self-confidence is destroyed and your reputation is ruined... or... you're dead."

"So," Roscoe said. "That's why you didn't back down from Jasper."

Clay nodded.

"Would you have shot him?"

Clay hesitated; he calculated the odds of these two fellows grasping the concept. "Yes," he said softly. "He was a deadly threat to both of us. If he'd taken another step toward us and started swingin' that pipe... yes... I would have pulled the trigger."

"You would have killed Jasper?" Marty exclaimed.

"He was gonna bash our heads in with a lead pipe," Clay replied. "It wasn't even us he was after in the first place. And I'm quite sure he wouldn't have hesitated to finish us off. What would y'all do?"

"I... I don't know," Marty said modestly. "I wasn't there."

"Sure seems like a lot of trouble to get a piano player," Christian laughed.

That seemed to lighten the serious nature of the conversation. He was tired of Jasper as the focal point; he was gone; Clay was the victor; it was time to get on with the business they came for.

Marty looked at Christian as if he had two heads. Then he glared at Roscoe. "What's he talkin' about, Roscoe?"

"They said they need a piano player."

Marty scowled at Christian and Clay again. "You mean... you rescued me from Jasper's gang because you need a piano player?"

"Well... yeah..." Christian replied. "But we weren't counting on Jasper when we came looking for you."

"How did you know where to find me?"

"We didn't... that's where Roscoe comes in."

"I've been at the lake fishing," Roscoe explained. "I met them at the Chateau last night. I told them about you."

"What gives you the right to stick your nose into my business?" Marty gave his friend a shove, and then lunged toward him.

Much smaller than either of them, Clay stepped

between them before Marty could do any more damage. "Take it easy, Marty!" he said, holding the aggressor back. "Y'all should consider yourself lucky that he did... or maybe you'd be layin' back there in that alley right now."

Marty knew he was acting irrationally; his temper—that he usually kept in check—was flaring only because he was experiencing an extremely bad day. He abruptly surrendered to Clay's intervention; a fist fight with Roscoe wouldn't solve anything.

"Listen," Christian said trying to calm him down. "We heard you're a pretty darn good pianist. It was us who wrangled Roscoe into coming to Baraboo to look for you, so don't blame him."

"So why do you need a pianist?" Marty said in a calmer tone.

"Well, you see, it's like this," Christian said putting a hand on Marty's shoulder and steering him off to the side, away from Roscoe. "We're part of a theater troupe..."

While Christian and Marty wandered off, Christian explaining how they came to Wisconsin without the rest of the actors and musicians, Roscoe and Clay found a bench in the shade of the depot.

"Are you really a professional gambler?" Roscoe asked.

"Was," Clay responded. "I made a good living at it. Guess y'all could call it that."

"But now you're an entertainer. Why did you quit gambling?"

"Poker was gettin' mighty risky out there in the

gold fields... too many hotheads with itchy trigger fingers... if y'all know what I mean."

Roscoe nodded. "And the hotheads were probably the usual losers at cards?"

"Y'all got it figured just about right... and 'cause I kinda take a liking to stay breathing a while longer, I decided to change my line o' work."

"But you're so quick with that gun—"

"The derringer y'all saw was only my backup. When we get back to the hotel, I'll show you the *equalizer*... my Smith n' Wesson forty-five."

"You carry a forty-five?"

"Not so much anymore... just the Remington derringer. It gives me a sense of safety."

"Will you teach me?" Roscoe said.

"What? To shoot?"

"No... cards. Poker."

Two hours seemed to flash by once good conversation took over. Other people started gathering on the boarding platform and then the faint sound of a whistle echoed. The eastbound was only ten minutes behind schedule, but the engineer and the conductor were determined to make up the lost time, somehow. Belching smoke and steam like the big iron monster it was, the engine rolled past the loading platform a little faster than usual. A frantic conductor nearly lost his cap as he stepped off the still moving cars. When the train finally came to an abrupt halt, he was already urging those waiting to get ready for boarding. Only a few passengers disembarked, and then the dozen people besides Clay, Christian, Roscoe and

Marty were hurriedly shuffled aboard. The routine fifteen-minute stop was reduced to ten.

It was impossible to shorten the stop at Baraboo with so many travelers getting off and on the train. Clay was confident that Jasper and his dogs would be nowhere in sight of the station, but he scanned the area through the car windows anyway. Roscoe leaned toward the window, his eyes searching the crowd. "Any sign of 'em?" he whispered.

"No," Clay replied. "I'm sure they've given up by now."

Marty and Christian were too busy talking about music and entertainment to demonstrate concern. Brief accounts of Marty's circus life the previous summer intrigued Christian, although Christian didn't think it was a life for him. "When we travel on the train," Marty enlightened, "performers and musicians have their own cars... men and women in separate cars, of course. Each person has their compartment... kinda like bunk beds. That's where you keep your personal belongings and where you sleep. Not much room, but you get used to it."

"We had our own theater," Christian said. "So we never traveled. But there were a lot of vaudeville acts that traveled to us. When we weren't performing, we were running the opera house."

"All aboard!" the conductor called out. The whistle sounded. The train jerked ahead and started rolling away from the station. They were finally on their way back to the lake.

FOUR

Although he hadn't done any fishing that day, Roscoe couldn't help but feel good about the outcome; he'd made some new friends, and his old friend, Marty Mason, had been saved from a terrible fate. And miraculously, he'd managed to navigate the search for Marty without his father discovering him back in town. Now that it was nearly suppertime, he remembered that he hadn't eaten since breakfast. But as the foursome walked to the *Cliff House* from the Devil's Lake depot, he wasn't the only one who was hungry. It had been a long, tiring day for them all.

At the supper table in the hotel dining hall, the conversation between Christian and Marty continued non-stop; Roscoe and Clay listened mostly:

33

"The circus came to Silver Spring," Christian said. "It was great... all the animals and clowns... and the horses! There was this one young girl who performed acrobatic stunts on a white galloping stallion! And the trapeze artists..." He went on like an excited little kid telling about the circus.

"Last summer," Marty said, "We had a band of pickpockets following us around... happens a lot with circuses. Police never did catch any of 'em."

That reminded Christian of another story: "Bank robbers hit the Silver Spring Bank during the closing parade. Me and my good friend Clancy saw the men go into the bank while we walked along with the band wagon. But we didn't think anything of it at the time... until the Town Marshal came looking. We'd seen those same men running away down an alley. When we told the Marshal about it, he knew who they were from our description."

"Did they catch 'em?" Roscoe asked.

"Well," Christian resumed. "That turned into a night I'll never forget. I got taken hostage by the bank robbers later at the hotel where I was singing."

"You were kidnapped?"

"Yeah... when the Marshal confronted one of them playing poker there, he grabbed me and held a gun to my head, dragging me out the door."

Clay had heard this story before so he managed to stay calm, but Marty and Roscoe were on the edge. Their eyes widened and they leaned in to hear every word Christian told about him and another bystander being used as shields to protect the outlaws in their retreat out of the hotel. "They drug us at gunpoint into the hardware store just down the street. But we broke away from them when they tried to steal a couple of horses there, and our good friend, Clancy, rescued me on his horse in the back alley... and he actually shot the crooks off the horses they were going to steal."

"Wow!" Marty exclaimed. "Did he kill 'em?"

"No, he just wounded them so they couldn't ride away, and then the marshal and his deputies captured them."

Roscoe and Marty were thrilled to be in the company of these new friends who had experienced firsthand the excitement of the gold and silver mining western frontier. They had read newspaper accounts of wild west episodes—bank and train robberies involving the likes of Jesse James, Butch Cassidy, and many other notorious outlaws, Indian uprisings, buffalo and cattle stampedes—all the things that kept the west a glorious and exciting place in the eyes of those who hadn't yet experienced it for themselves. Marty and Roscoe had never rubbed elbows with anyone who actually had.

Clay had been waiting for the right opportunity to question Marty about his run-in with Jasper's gang. "Why," he asked, "was Jasper so intent on making you a bloody mess?"

"Oh, that," replied Marty. He gave a sheepish little grin and his freckled cheeks turned a bit red. "I just suggested that he could get a job as a clown in the Ringling Circus."

"And for that y'all just about became a pile of chop suey?"

Marty nodded. "Yeah. I was just trying to be helpful, but I guess it doesn't take much to get Jasper all riled up."

When they had finished their pork chops, potatoes and gravy, they realized they were the last ones left in the dining hall. Because the hotel wasn't full yet at this time of year, there had been a small supper crowd, and everyone else had already left. "Hey, Marty," Christian said. "How 'bout giving me a little sample of your piano playing?"

"Where are we gonna find a piano?" Marty asked.

"Oh... we have a piano. It's in the extra room Simon rented to store all our theater gear."

"You brought a piano with you to the hotel?"

"Well... yeah... we couldn't just leave it behind."

The extra room was in the back of the hotel, between Simon's room and the one occupied by him and Clay. Christian kept a key. He opened the door and they all went in, although there wasn't much empty space among all the trunks and wooden crates.

"What *is* all this stuff?" Roscoe asked.

"Costumes and props, mostly," Christian replied. "Some of it is Simon's personal belongings, and those long rolls of canvas are stage backdrops... with scenery painted on them."

The bed had been pushed into one corner to make more room, and beside it stood the upright pi-

ano, a thin layer of dust covering its otherwise polished mahogany finish. Christian shoved a couple of
trunks aside to give access to the keyboard, and then
gestured to Marty as if he were giving a sacrifice to a
God.

Marty's freckled face beamed as he lifted the
keyboard cover and pulled back the stool. Then his
fingers danced across the ivory and a few bars of a
lively circus march filled the room, followed by the
familiar *Man on the Flying Trapeze*.

Christian smiled and looked at Clay. "It's a little
different than Fingers' style, but we can work on it."
Then he tapped Marty on the shoulder. "Do you know
Sunny Side of the Street?"

Marty stopped playing abruptly, bobbed his head
a few times as he thought, and then stumbled a little
on the melody with his right hand, but within a short
time the full harmonious sound had Christian singing
the lyrics.

Clay didn't need to hear any more; he was convinced that Marty was an accomplished musician. He
turned to Roscoe. "Y'all wanna go next door and play
some cards?"

FIVE

It had been nearly midnight when Roscoe and Marty went off to Roscoe's room. Marty was adjusting to a vaudeville piano style, and Roscoe had learned the value of a poker face, and that a full house was a pretty good hand. But they both had a ways to go yet.

The next morning, Clay and Christian looked for their new friends at breakfast. Roscoe, however, was an early riser; he had already wandered out to the lake with his fishing gear, trying to make up for lost time, and he already had two very nice bass on his stringer. Marty, though, came sauntering into the dining hall, sleepy-eyed, just as the other two were well into platefuls of scrambled eggs, fried potatoes, and bacon. He stood silently by their table, as if waiting for an invitation to sit down.

"Good morning, Marty," Christian greeted.

"Won't you join us?"

"Mornin'" Marty responded, pulled out a chair and sat down.

"Are y'all havin' breakfast?" Clay asked.

"I... I... don't have any money with me," Marty said. "I left town yesterday in a bit of a hurry..."

"Yeah, we know." Clay waved to a passing waitress. "Would y'all please bring my friend a breakfast plate? I'll pay for it."

"Thank you," Marty said sheepishly after the waitress had left. "You really didn't have to do that."

"Sure I did. Y'all are hungry. Can't stand to see a friend go hungry."

"Why are you being so kind to me?" Marty asked. "You saved my skin back in that alley; you treated me to supper last night; and now breakfast..."

Clay saw that satisfying twinkle in Christian's eyes; he knew how much Christian wanted to be performing again, and he knew how he appreciated a *good* piano player for his accompaniment. Apparently he was enthused by Marty's ability. "Well, let's just put it this way, Marty," he said with a gleam in his eye. "We kinda like you, and now that I've risked my reputation... almost havin' to shoot someone because of y'all... I guess I just wanna protect my investment." He grinned.

"Um, that's what I wanted to talk to you about this morning," Marty said. But then the waitress interrupted him as she set a steaming hot plate of food in front of him. He eyed it with appreciation. "Thank you," he said to the waitress as she turned to leave, and then, as if embarrassed to make his request, he stared at the center of the table as he continued. "I... I was kinda wondering if I could hang out here with you for a few days... until Jasper cools off... I mean... I'll pay you back for the room and the food and all... I have money back at my Ma's house... but if I go back there now I know Jasper will be watchin' for me... and you must've seen what kind of guy he is."

Clay frowned. "Are y'all saying that you want me to be your bodyguard?"

"No... no... not at all... well, maybe... but Jasper's not smart enough to come out here looking for me."

Christian washed down his last bite of potatoes with a gulp of cold milk. "But we were hoping that you'd stay on with us anyway... join our troupe. You're the best piano player we've seen since we left Silver Spring."

Marty's expression turned solemn. "But I've got a job with the Ringling Circus."

Christian's face drooped as if every last bit of good in the world had drained away. This had been his only hope in several months to have a talented musician join them, and now that hope was melting.

Marty noticed his dismay. "All right... I'll play for you until the circus people get back."

"When's that?"

"First of May."

"Well, that's less than a month... but it's a start," Christian said. His good spirit partially returned. "You might change your mind after you get a taste of vaudeville. I think it might be a little better lifestyle than the circus... from what you told me yesterday. And you're gonna like Simon."

At three o'clock that afternoon the *Chicago & North Western* delivered about forty vacationers at the Devil's Lake depot. Among them was Simon Bordeaux returning from one of his frequent scouting trips, and accompanying him were Claudia and Vivian Moon, who had been actresses in the troupe back in Silver Spring. By chance, Simon had run across the Moon sisters in Chicago; they were headed to New York, as their thrill of the West had worn thin. But Simon convinced them to give Wisconsin a try. "Christian and Clay are there with me," he had told them. He knew they were rather fond of the two young actors. "All right," they finally gave in. "What could it hurt? We'll give it a whirl." And so then, Simon's theater troupe was about to be partially reunited; and if some of the others who had responded to his telegrams and letters could find their way to Devil's Lake Village, he would soon have nearly a full complement of actors and musicians.

As Simon approached his hotel room door he heard the piano in the storage room. He was quite sure that Christian had the only other key, and Christian couldn't play the piano—not like that! And then he heard Christian's singing voice, so he had to be in there with someone who could. Simon tried the door; it was unlocked. Standing in the doorway, he watched and listened to the duo with their backs to him, unaware that he was there. *After the Ball* sounded as good now as it ever had at the Crystal Palace in Silver Spring. Obviously, Christian had found a piano player.

"You two must've been rehearsing a long time," Simon said as he clapped his hands in appreciation of what he had just heard.

Christian and Marty spun around, startled by Simon's voice. Christian stepped briskly to the door to greet Simon. "Hi, Simon! Welcome back. Did you have a good trip?"

"Yes, actually, I did... and you'll never guess who I found in Chicago."

"Who?"

"Claudia and Vivian... they're checking into a room right now."

"Claudia and Vivian are here?"

Simon nodded and then glanced toward the piano player. "And who's this you've been rehearsing with?"

"Oh! Yes! This is Marty Mason," Christian said as he led Simon to the piano. "Marty? This is Simon Bordeaux."

"Pleased to meet you, Mr. Bordeaux," the freckle-faced lad said as he shook Simon's hand.

"Marty played with the Ringling Circus last season," Christian explained. "And we've only been tryin' out a few songs for the last couple of hours. Clay and I just met him yesterday."

"Where is that rascal, Clay?" Simon asked.

"Oh, I think he's out fishing with Roscoe."

"Who's Roscoe?"

"Marty's friend. We actually met him first, and he told us about Marty."

Simon examined Marty's less-than-fashionable attire as if he were choosing a puppy from a litter. "Well, I suppose we can groom him a bit."

"Marty's here as the result of a hasty maneuver," Christian said. "So he didn't have time to get dressed up."

"And where do you call home?" Simon asked.

"Baraboo," Marty replied.

"You were a windjammer with the Ringlings."

"Yes sir."

"A *forty-miler*, no doubt."

"No, sir," Marty said proudly. "I was *with it*... stayed the whole season."

"What's a *forty-miler?*" asked Christian.

Marty explained: "That's what the other performers call you if they think you're not gonna make it. But I was *with it*... didn't quit."

Christian eyed Simon curiously. "How do you know all this lingo?"

"I've been in show business nearly all my life... talked to a lot of circus people."

SIX

Warmer weather was beginning to attract more people to the lake; the lodges were filling with vacationers at a steady pace, and the private cottages showed signs of awakening. With every train arrival, Simon anxiously awaited the appearance of his troupe members. One by one, they started showing up—Henry Holland, the drummer; Victor Abbot, an actor; Clyde Cameron, the violinist, comedian and actor; Charlotte Van Horn, a singer, dancer, and actress—and there would be others. Christian and Clay saw Simon's confidence building and they knew they would soon be back on the stage.

Even though Marty didn't know any of the returning troupe, he could sense Christian's energy and enthusiasm—the kind of energy he had felt performing at circus shows. But this seemed different, some-how; in the circus, he was just one little digit among a multitude, blending his presence and talent with so many others that he was barely noticed. Here, though, Christian and Clay were stars among a much smaller group—a group in which every member shone as a significant player, contributing their indi-vidual character that everyone noticed. *Perhaps this was the very element that Christian meant,* Marty thought, *when he tried to convince me that I'd be happier here... or... sleeping in a hotel bed every night instead of a crowded, rumbling rail car amidst the putrid odor of sweat and stinky feet of fifty other men, and bathing in a hotel bathtub instead of an oc-casional bucket bath.*

In all honesty, Marty did enjoy traveling with the circus, even though the traveling accommodations weren't the most pleasant. His space on the train car had been a four-foot-by-six-foot compartment with its "crumb box"—a small storage space for his personal belongings. The compartment served as his bunk, that, occasionally he had to share with another *First of May*—a newcomer—or *Forty-miler.* The shar-ing usually didn't last long, as most of the newcom-ers didn't last. They were quickly labeled a *Forty-miler* when it became evident they couldn't cope with the lifestyle of the circus, and then they would soon be gone, leaving Marty the full expanse of his tiny dwelling again.

But now there was a new option looming before him: Christian seemed to appreciate his musical talent, and if the singer could convince Simon, the master of the organization, to let Marty join the troupe, he could say good-bye to the tiny sleeping compartment on the train car. *Is that what I want?* he thought. *Do I want to say good-bye to all the friends I made there? Do I want to leave that exciting life of the circus and the thrill of seeing new places?* It would be a tough decision, perhaps.

Marty had a couple of weeks to make up his mind. He'd have to be certain that he was compatible with this new "family" and that they would readily accept him. He wasn't at all concerned about the pay; Christian and Clay appeared to be financially well-endowed, and Simon Bordeaux seemed to have not a care in the world; he could afford to travel to far-away cities, stay in luxury hotels, and wear the finest clothes. No, Marty wasn't concerned about the potential earnings.

There was, however, one other concern that merited consideration. Now that his home base would be Baraboo again, it could not be ignored. As long as he had been traveling with the circus, away most of the time, and when he wasn't away, Marty had been shrouded by the circus people, able to remain out of reach by his nemesis... Jasper Blackburn. They had been arch-rivals for as long as Marty could remember, and just a few days ago, Marty had renewed the rivalry by attempting to resolve it—by suggesting to Jasper the possibility of a job with the circus. His intentions had been sincere, but Jasper Adler had misinterpreted the offer of being a circus clown as an insult. Marty's scheme to try befriending his enemy had kicked back like a stubborn mule and had almost gotten him killed.

Thanks to his good friend, Roscoe, he was saved from that horrible doom, although Clay Edwards had played the key role, and because of that, Clay gave him a feeling of security. The ex-gambler wasn't afraid of Jasper, or at least he knew how to summon up the courage to defend against the bully. And now that Jasper knew about Clay, maybe there wouldn't be any more trouble.

Clay spent a lot of time with Roscoe during his week at the lake. Other than his friendship with Marty Mason, Roscoe seemed more a loner, although he also seemed to know nearly everyone who lived in Baraboo. Familiarity with so many people stemmed from working in his father's store; he'd never had any trouble making acquaintances, but seldom did he wish to spend longer periods of time than a casual, passing conversation with any of them. But Clay was different, just like Marty had been different. Marty was always the courageous one, always ready and eager for some new adventure, and Roscoe was usually quiet and more recluse. But their personalities fit together like bacon and eggs. Marty had tried to convince Roscoe to join the circus a year ago, and it might have happened, but Roscoe's father put a stop to it. They had been close friends since their early school days, and Roscoe might have preferred accompanying Marty on the circus trail, however, being the obedient son, he remained loyal to the family business. Staying in his father's good graces seemed the right thing to do at the time.

Now there was Clay. In some respects, he was much like Marty—genuinely friendly, but in that warm, southern biscuits and gravy sort of friendly that was difficult not to like. Clay was bold; he, too, had ventured out on his own from a small Mississippi town that folks in other parts of the country had never heard of. At only sixteen, he had left his home and family in Mississippi, making his life the way he chose. There was no reason to doubt that he had actually gained his apparent wealth by gambling; he was exceptionally good at poker, and his swiftness with a gun was unmatched by anyone Roscoe knew. That didn't make him an outlaw, as first impressions had led Roscoe and Marty to believe in the alley in Baraboo, but it still did cause some curious thoughts.

SEVEN

I t was a gray day. The fish weren't biting. Roscoe had only one more day at the lake after this one. He gazed up at the overcast sky, wondering if Clay would once again join him, as he had the previous three days. His new friend had been good companionship whiling away the time waiting for the big ones to take their bait.

All along the rocky shoreline, other anglers were having no more luck than he was; perhaps it would be a good day to do something else. So what if he missed a few more hours of fishing? He thought of hiking into the bluffs overlooking the lake, to view the breathtaking panorama. That had always been one of his favorite pastimes when there was nothing better to do. And maybe he could go to the hotel first, and ask Clay to join him on the hike.

Dozens of vacationers had just arrived at the Cliff House via the train; it was a madhouse, people pushing and crowding, tripping over each other's baggage trying to get to the registration desk. Roscoe skirted around the small mob of impatient guests and headed to the back of the hotel where he thought he would find the others, perhaps rehearsing some musical numbers. He found Christian alone in the extra room with the piano. "Where is everybody?" he asked.

Christian looked up from the sheet music he had been practicing. "Marty and Simon are having a private discussion."

"Private?"

"Yeah... I think Simon is making Marty an offer."

"Offer?"

"Yeah... to join our troupe."

"Oh. Think he will?"

"Don't know," Christian said. "Hope so. He's a good pianist. Thanks for introducing us."

"Sure," Roscoe replied. "So, where's Clay?"

Christian peered past Roscoe toward the open door. "I thought he was with you. He left here a half-hour ago to look for you at the lake."

"I... I must've missed him. The fishing's no good today so I came back, and I was on the opposite side of the lake today."

"He said he would walk the shoreline down to the Kirkland Hotel. If he didn't find you along the way, he'd ride the boat back here."

Roscoe looked at his pocket watch. It was already past two o'clolck. He remembered seeing the *Capitola* at the dock, the crew building steam. "I think the boat is leaving here soon, so I guess I'll get on it."

"You'll be sure to find him, then."

Roscoe hurried down to the dock. Dark gray smoke boiled from the smokestack of the *Capitola*, the small steam powered excursion boat that gave vacationers a leisurely cruise around the lake, and often delivered travelers to the *Cliff House* from the train depot. On Saturday afternoons during the summer, it ferried passengers from the South Shore hotels to the North Shore *Chateau* shows and dances. A trim little vessel, the *Capitola* could comfortably carry about fifteen or twenty passengers; Roscoe counted only a half-dozen or so on the dock waiting to board.

"Will you be stopping at the Kirkland dock?" he asked the boat captain as he approached.

The boatman nodded. "Will you be getting off there?"

"No... well, maybe, but a friend might be waiting there to get on."

"Okay," the captain said. "Have a seat and enjoy the ride."

The side paddlewheels started churning the water and the sturdy little steamer puffed away from the dock, navigating along the East side of the lake about fifty yards out from the shore. This was a new experience for Roscoe; the many times he had visited Devil's Lake, he had never taken the *Capitola* cruise. It sure beat rowing a skiff, as he sometimes did when he came here to fish. Now it was just a matter of sitting back, relaxing, and keeping an eye on the shoreline hopeful to spot Clay. In the meantime, he had time to think about what decision Marty would make about leaving the circus to join a band of strangers he hardly knew.

Back at the hotel, that very decision was being discussed. Simon had auditioned Marty Mason, and he had heard him play accompaniment for a few of Christian's songs; so far, he liked what he heard, although Marty needed a little grooming—both in physical appearance and his musical style. He had to gain some elegance in his dress, and he had to lose the circus flair at the keyboard. In time it would all come around.

When Simon invited him to a private conversation, Marty didn't know exactly what to expect; it would either be rejection or persuasion to become part of this show. If it was rejection, he still had his job with the Ringling Circus, and if it was persuasion, he wasn't ready to make a commitment just yet. He liked Christian and Clay, and Simon seemed to be a likeable sort, too. But he had only met briefly the rest of the group and he hadn't gotten to know them very well.

"I'm sure by now," Simon began, "that Christian has informed you all about our theater troupe."

"Well, he's told me some, yes."

"And has he said anything about you joining us?"

"Yes... yes, he has mentioned it."

"Good," Simon said. "Then this won't be a complete surprise to you. Have you given some thought to the idea?"

"A little... but I haven't made any decisions yet. Are you saying that you want me to stay?"

"Yes, I want you to stay with us. I think you belong with us."

"But I really don't know any of the others. What if they don't like me?"

"You know Christian and Clay, and they seem to like you."

"Well... yeah... but the others..."

"Did you know everyone in the circus before you joined them?"

"No... but—"

"I wouldn't worry about the others. They all adore Christian and Clay, and they'll like you, as well."

"How can you be so sure?"

"I know my people," Simon declared. "And I recognize your talent as a musician, and so do they."

"I'll have to think about it," Marty said. He was being cautious.

"What are you so unsure of, Marty?" Simon asked.

"That I won't fit in... I won't be good enough."

"I already know that you're good enough, Marty. All you need is a little polish."

"But if I feel bullied or abused in any way, I'm gone."

"I will... we *all* will... do our best to keep you from

feeling that way," said Simon. "But if you choose to stay, you will have to abide by my rules. We're a company. We have procedures and laws, much like you experienced traveling with the circus. We all pull together as a team, and everyone works his share, and everyone is treated equally."

"I don't expect any favoritism," Marty said.

"And you won't get any. However, I will expect perfection from you. The pianist plays a very important roll, and I think you understand that."

Marty smiled. For the first time since Christian had praised his performance, he felt a sense of pride heating up inside.

"So, will you stay with us?" Simon asked again.

"Let me sleep on it."

At the other end of the lake, the little steamer, *Capitola*, was nearing the South Shore dock. Roscoe spotted Clay walking along the bank. He stood up on the boat deck, waved his arms over his head and called out: "CLAY!"

Clay heard the call and looked toward the boat. When he noticed Roscoe, he returned the wave. "I'LL MEET YOU AT THE DOCK."

The grayness of the day didn't seem quite so dreary as the two friends met. "Not out fishin' today?" Clay asked.

"They weren't biting, so I thought I'd see if you were interested in a hike up to the bluffs." Roscoe's voice had an overtone of cordiality.

Clay balanced his companion's proposal for an

indecisive moment, focused his gaze to the tops of the hills surrounding the lake. "Up there?"

"Yeah," Roscoe replied. "The view is fantastic."

"Should we see if Marty and Christian want to join us?"

"Just came from the hotel," Roscoe said. "They're kinda busy right now."

"Well, then... lead the way."

EIGHT

The climb to the top of the rocky bluff was quite demanding, but Clay finally admitted that it was worth the effort. He had grumbled a bit during the long, strenuous climb, but when the amazing vista lay before him with the lake far below, he changed his tune. Even on this dismal, gray day, the view was breathtaking, just as Roscoe had said it would be.

They sat on some high boulders gazing at the scenery, neither one speaking. Because the weather was less than favorable for hikers, they were alone.

Roscoe finally broke the silence. "So, what was that town in Montana really like?"

"Silver Spring?" Clay replied. "It was no sleepy little town... a wild and uncurried timber wolf, and it howled every night."

"Howled?"

"The streets were lined with more saloons and gambling halls than y'all can imagine, and they were full every night... miners and cattlemen and lumber-men, drinking and gambling their money away, and they *weren't* a quiet bunch. Payrolls were large, and there were plenty of gamblers, gunmen, and thieves gathered for the pickings."

"You gambled in those places, too?"

"Not all of 'em... just a couple. Occasionally at Tanglewood Lodge, but mostly at the Royal Hotel. They were classier joints, higher stakes, and not so many rowdies."

"Rowdies? Like Jasper?"

"Roscoe, my friend... Jasper is a toddler com-pared to the rowdies I'm talkin' about. In Silver Spring, just about everybody carried a gun, and they drank whiskey like y'all drink water. It would be an odd day to walk down the street and not see at least one fist-fight, and maybe some gunplay."

"Didn't the police try to keep a lid on all that?" Roscoe asked.

"Police? We only had one Town Marshal... Flana-gan... and he did what he could. But keepin' a lid on *all* the drunken disputes was somewhere between a bad idea and impossible."

"Sounds like a real nasty place."

"Actually," Clay smiled. "Silver Spring was next to paradise."

"How can you call a place like that paradise?"

"Because... for the most part, all the people

there—besides the rowdies—were kind and friendly; Silver Spring was nestled in the mountain foothills, and it was a lot like here, except instead of a lake, we had a small river, an' just like here, a prettier place would be hard to find. Everybody there had plenty of money and lived comfortably. Life was good there."

"If you ever go back there," Roscoe said. "Could I go with you?"

"Don't reckon anybody will ever go back to Silver Spring, Roscoe. We got letters over the winter from Clancy, our last friend there; he told us that the whole town was destroyed by fire after we left. Ain't nobody there anymore."

"The entire town is gone?"

"Yup... according to Clancy."

"Wow... hard to imagine a whole town disappearing."

"I guess me and Christian got out of there just in time."

"So, how did you and Christian meet?"

"Christian worked for Silas Patch, the proprietor of the Royal Hotel. He'd escort travelers from the railroad depot to the hotel and carry their baggage on a cart. Just about everybody arriving at Silver Spring ended up at either the Royal or Tanglewood, depending on which messenger got to them first— Christian, from the Royal, or Clancy, from Tanglewood. Anyhow, that's where I first met Christian. He took me to the Royal to get a room, and after that we happened to bump into each other a few times around the saloon and gambling hall. One

61

evening, he invited me to join him at his table for supper, and we became good friends."

"D'ya think he'll get Mason to quit the circus?"

"I'd say the chances are good."

The corners of Roscoe's mouth curled into a little smile; he hadn't liked it when his best friend ran off with the circus, leaving him to spend most of the last summer alone.

"It'll be gettin' dark early... with this cloud cover," Clay said looking up into the grayness. "Maybe we ought to start back."

Roscoe led the way down the steep trail back to the lake. It was dusk; the warm air of the early spring afternoon was being crowded by an exhilarating evening chill. In the half-light the golden beach sand acquired the smooth texture of a thick carpet, spreading out to the thin woods, and down to the shimmering lake with the stolid little steamer perched beside the long, narrow, jutting dock. Beyond, the landscape sloped gently up, dissected by the railroad tracks, and to the gray square shape of the hotel, and then the wooded hills rose abruptly forming the high horizon against the darkening gray sky.

"See y'all at supper tonight?" Clay asked as they were about to part.

"Yeah," replied Roscoe. "It'll be my last one with you... I have to go back home tomorrow afternoon."

Unbeknownst to Clay, supper that evening was to be a gala affair; Simon had invited all the returned cast members to join him in the dining hall, and he insisted that Marty Mason be there, too, even though he wasn't officially a part of the troupe yet. "It will give you a chance to get to know them better," he told the pianist. "You have to start somewhere."

Marty hesitantly accepted the invitation; he didn't know the reason for his reluctance, but he was determined to figure it out during a solo walk along the lakeshore. As he stepped onto the gravel path that led over the railroad tracks, he felt strong and durable with the sound of his boots on the hard surface. But he sensed once again that he was helplessly sliding back into the foggy social bottomland where beginners dwell. Not that he was an outcast; all the time he had been with the circus, he had never been treated adversely by the other windjammers, nor had it ever been suggested that he gather his belongings and determine the next appropriate jumping-off spot to exit the train. Such victims *were* genuine outcasts. But that was not Marty. He had actually gained a couple of rungs on the social ladder among the circus people, and he had succeeded in becoming accepted and even respected by the entire band.

He stepped cautiously along the trail, only a few feet from the water's edge, suddenly realizing the trees were mere silhouettes and the dusky chill added to the already dreary conditions would soon devour everything in darkness. The lake surface magnified and reflected what little light was left; Marty stopped and stared at it. "Am I doing the right thing? Leaving the circus and joining this bunch I don't really know?"

he asked, as if he expected a reply from some unseen spirit. Taking a deep breath of the cool, refreshing air and then sighing, he remembered once again that he had merely inhabited that nether world of the un-regarded where no one bothered him or bothered about him. In the circus band he had just been one small integer of the body, rarely recognized as any-thing significant. Being a part of Simon Bordeaux's theater troupe, however, he could advance to the sta-tus of a star performer. The thought of it was intoxi-cating. Visions swirled in his head: he, Marty Mason, dressed in a fine tuxedo, bowing in the footlights be-fore an appreciative crowd after a brilliant perfor-mance. What more could he possibly want?

Standing there staring into the water, motionless, he suddenly felt a shiver in his bones as he gradually slipped back into reality. He wasn't certain how long he had been standing there in that daze, but now darkness had swallowed everything. The lights from the Chateau gave him direction, and then the warm, friendly glow from the hotel reminded him that he was expected in the dining room. Exercising willpow-er, he walked, holding himself back from running; he didn't want to appear out of breath when he arrived at the supper table.

NINE

Adorned with appointments characteristic of such inns—polished walnut woodwork, the tan and green wallpaper depicting Colonial scenes, and a friendly fireplace—the dining room purred with the many quiet conversations by an increasing number of guests. At the far end of the room, Marty saw his supper partners huddled at a large corner table. He strode past other tables, bright with white linens and silver, aware of the murmuring groups here and there, but his focus was on the far corner table. He was surprised to see Roscoe there, sitting next to Clay; Roscoe appeared to feel out of place, and rightly so, among all the actors and musicians. But Marty was glad Roscoe was there; it perhaps seemed as though he had been ignoring his best friend the entire week, spending most of the time with Christian.

It was Roscoe who first noticed Marty's approach. He nudged Clay and nodded toward Marty. Clay, in turn, patted Simon's shoulder.

Simon looked up, eyeing Marty dressed in the clothes he had borrowed from Roscoe. "For Heaven's sake," he whispered to Christian. "I thought you were going to get him a jacket from our wardrobe."

"I did," Christian responded. "But he disappeared before I could get it to him."

"Well, take him back and dress him properly for dining."

Christian rose from his chair and met Marty before he reached the table. "Come with me," he said as he turned Marty around and started walking him out. "We're going to get you into some different clothes."

"Why do I need different clothes?" Marty whispered.

"Didn't you see everyone else at the table? Even Roscoe has a coat and tie."

"Why is Roscoe there?"

"Clay invited him. And where were you? We were beginning to wonder if you were gonna show up."

"I was out walking... thinking some things out. You and Mr. Bordeaux are asking me to make a big decision, y' know."

Christian opened the storeroom door and urged Marty inside; they had spent so much time there rehearsing at the piano that it didn't seem uncommon to be there. Marty watched as Christian gathered the garments he had picked out earlier.

"Why did Clay invite Roscoe?"

"This is Roscoe's last night here," Christian replied. "Clay invited him to supper before he knew about the party." He offered Marty the shirt and tie. "Put these on."

"Sometimes I wonder about Clay," Marty said as he slipped out of his old shirt and into the new. "Roscoe has told me a little about him, but he seems so mysterious to me... like he's hiding his past."

Christian looked Marty in the eyes. "I've come to know him quite well, and although it's true that Clay has some dark days in his past, he's not trying to hide anything. He's a Southern gentleman by instinct, of exceptionally good manners, and mild-tempered until provoked... and then, for God's sake, *look out.* He's absolutely fearless, but he's not a trouble hunter. Clay has a lot of natural ability and practices good common sense. No matter what you're thinking, there is nothing low about Clay Edwards. He's high-toned, broad-minded, cool-headed, and brave. And as you *should* know from recent experience, he's a good guy to have on your side."

He helped straighten the tie, handed over the vest, and then held the jacket open for Marty to slip his arms into the sleeves.

When they returned to the dining hall, the table had been laden with a feast, and the pianist had transformed from a boy in ill-fitting street clothes to a dapper young man fit for a formal ball in long-tailed burgundy coat with satin lapels, matching vest, white shirt and black bowtie. He and Christian ushered themselves to the two vacant chairs next to Clay as the others' eyes followed the new lad, evaluating his appearance, although they knew the suit of clothes came from the theater's wardrobe. Marty felt a little uncomfortable at first, knowing all eyes were fixed on him.

"Everyone!" Simon announced. "Let us welcome our guests... Marty Mason, whom most of you have met, and Clay's friend, Roscoe."

Roscoe's cheeks reddened a little as he looked down into the tablecloth. He *was* out of place among this group and he knew it; the thought had crossed his mind to ask to be excused, but now everyone greeted him as though he belonged there, and the succulent roast pork, baked yams, and vegetable soup looked and smelled too good to walk away from, so he decided he would stay. Although he was clearly not interested in any of them beyond sharing a social supper table, the elite group made him feel welcome.

Marty's comfort level abruptly raised as he scanned all the faces around the table that were no longer staring, but seemed warm and friendly toward him and Roscoe, even though Roscoe had no real purpose there. Marty had to measure his capacity for self-discipline. Now it seemed apparent that he could turn his back on the circus, but he could not allow himself to be entangled in cheap competition for importance. He had to embrace this opportunity with exceeding intelligence.

"I've been told you're a splendid piano man," Charlotte Van Horn said, batting her eyes just enough to suggest she might be interested in the new arrival. She was one from the group Marty had not met, although Christian had informed him that she was an actress, dancer, and singer. That would account for her concern of his musical ability.

Before Marty had a chance to reply to Charlotte's remark, Henry Holland and Clyde Cameron chimed in: "We must get together sometime soon for a practice session."

Among all the other welcoming comments and greetings, it seemed to Marty that everyone there had reached the assumption that he was already a member of the troupe, and he wasn't quite sure how to react. But he was certain that he felt more thoroughly aware, now, of how the world worked—of who fit where, of what was grand and genuine, and what was shoddy and fake. He had joined the circus a year ago for the excitement and adventure. But the circus was filled with illusions, like the ferocious lions that weren't really ferocious at all—they were as tame as kittens—but they were well-trained to make the audience *believe* they were ferocious. The Fat Lady really weighed only 400 pounds, but to an unsuspecting circus audience, she was the world's fattest woman at 698. People believed they would witness the five-legged calf and the two-headed goat walking around in a pen inside the closed tent, when in reality they found on display deformed unborn fetuses preserved in formaldehyde and sealed in large glass jars. It all made for good entertainment, perhaps, but illusions, just the same.

There was nothing that appeared fake or dishonest about this group; Christian and Clay had been straightforward right from the beginning; Simon Bordeaux had laid his cards on the table along with his rules and honest expectations; and so far, nothing had aroused any suspicions about the others. Deep in reflective thought, Marty stirred his soup. He felt his true ambitions coming into focus as he envisioned himself as the majestic musician. He decided instinctively to accept Simon's offer, right there at the supper table, among the white linens, walnut, and silver, and the polite whispers and nods of the others.

"Ladies and gentlemen," Marty spoke up. He peered at all the faces; when it seemed he had their attention, he went on. "A couple of days ago, Mr. Bordeaux asked me to join your theater group as a pianist. I didn't give him an answer then, and I haven't yet. As you probably know by now, I traveled with the Ringling Circus last summer, so I'm not exactly a stranger to show business."

The others followed this unwinding of the new guy, carefully gauging his attitude and measured him according to their own rather critical yardsticks.

"None of you know me," Marty went on. "And I know none of you... well... except for Christian and Clay; they're the reason I'm here. They have chosen to have faith in me, and if the rest of you will share that sentiment, I can be the best piano man this troupe has ever known."

A few eyebrows lifted; Christian and Clay noticed. Simon Bordeaux noticed. Had Marty overstepped the boundaries of his welcome?

"What he means to say," Christian added, in an attempt to appease the ill feelings that may have been incubated by Marty's address, "is that he's willing to try to give us his best."

A few nods and half-smiles gave Christian the impression that that had been an acceptable revision of Marty's statement, but it was hard to totally assess the reaction as everyone had begun to enjoy the meal, paying more attention to the food rather than conversation.

When the meal was finished, the ladies of the group—Claudia and Vivian Moon, and Charlotte van Horn—excused themselves and delicately meandered across the room toward the exit. Clyde Cameron and Henry Holland soon followed, while Simon and Victor quietly discussed the selection of a new play. Nothing more had been said about Marty's boastful remark and he had been included in several discussions; Christian hoped that it would be soon forgotten.

Clay and Christian excused themselves, as did Marty; Roscoe just nodded his gratitude to Simon for the wonderful supper and followed the others out into the damp April night, around the corner where lights streamed warmly from cozy hotel room windows.

"So, Marty," Christian said. "Now it's official... you've been adopted. Will I see you for some rehearsal tomorrow? I can give you the sheet music for some of Charlotte's numbers."

"Yeah, okay..."

"Well, g'night," said Clay, as though he were passively bidding a "call" during a dull poker game.

"See you in the morning," Christian added as he and Clay headed for their room, leaving Marty and Roscoe to go their way.

Roscoe raised his open palm in a little wave, and then he turned to Marty. "Mason," he said. "I don't know about you, but I'm gonna get some sleep. I wanna get in some early morning fishing before I hafta leave tomorrow."

Marty just nodded as they started walking. He didn't know how he should feel; now that he was officially a member of Simon's theater troupe, he thought he should be celebrating, but instead, he was going to bed early. At least he wasn't climbing the dark stairway to the lonely little room stuck up under the eaves at his mother's house. "What time you goin' back tomorrow?"

"Thought I'd catch the two o'clock train."

"I'm goin' with you. Ma's prob'ly worried sick."

"You could take the morning train," Roscoe suggested.

"No... I wanna go with you."

TEN

After the fog lifted, clouds still painted the morning heavens in a dreary, somber gray with only a hint here and there that a blue sky did really exist. Roscoe kept hoping for a little sunshine on his last day at the lake; the fish might be biting a little better. Even though he had five nice Northerns waiting for him at the ice house, one more wouldn't hurt.

In the piano room, Marty seemed eager enough to begin rehearsals with the other singers and actors, but a trip to Baraboo seemed important to him, too. "I really need to go see my ma," he told Christian. "She's prob'ly worried by now... and besides... I'm still wearing the clothes I borrowed from Connor."

"When are you leaving?"

"This afternoon... I'm goin' on the train with Connor."

"So, when will you be back?" Christian asked.

"Monday. I'll come back Monday. First afternoon train."

"Why do you two always call each other by your last names?"

"Don't know... always have."

By one forty-five Roscoe Connor had retrieved his five chilled Northerns from the ice house and was waiting at the depot for the two o'clock train. "Great!" he said to himself. "*Now* the clouds start clearing." But it was too late to go back out fishing; he had his ticket in hand. He just marveled at the wonderfully pleasant afternoon as it unfurled before him, the sun patches growing and spreading as the clouds rolled away over the hills. He didn't feel disappointment, for he'd had a good week in spite of the interruptions. One day lost to a hunting excursion for his best friend, Mason, and a few late nights spent with new friends that hindered early morning rising was probably all worth the new friend he had made in Clay Edwards. Even though he might have little opportunity to ever spend more time with him, Clay had taught him the art of poker, and how to be a gentleman in Southern style that would surely astound his peers. Roscoe was eager to spend some of his savings for a new suit and shirts and ties like Clay wore. Perhaps he would still have time that afternoon... if the train wasn't late.

With only a few minutes to spare, Christian and Clay escorted Marty Mason to the depot platform.

"Hey, Mason," Roscoe greeted his friend. "I was beginning to wonder if you'd make it."

"Hey, Connor. Christian and I were going over some of the music for the show. If Clay hadn't come around to remind us, we'd prob'ly still be there."

"Hi, Clay," Roscoe smiled. "What would these guys do without you?"

Clay laughed. "They'd miss a lot of trains."

Marty turned to Christian. "Y' know... at first I was a little skeptical about leaving the circus and joining your troupe..."

"A little?" Christian grinned. "You were like trying to move the Rock of Gibraltar with a wheelbarrow."

"Well, I know I was a little difficult then, but I'm glad to be with you now... and I'm really anxious to start rehearsals."

"We're glad to have you... and you have no idea how anxious we are to get started again. Monday won't come too soon."

The big, black, smoking, engine rumbled slowly past them, steam hissing, bell clanging, and brakes squealing, delivering the passenger coaches to a stop at the platform. The foursome watched what seemed to be the entire population of Chicago disembarking the train. They made their parting handshakes, and as Marty and Roscoe stepped aboard the coach, Roscoe turned with a sorrowful expression and waved to Clay. "Come and see me at the store sometime," he called out.

Settled into their seats, Marty and Roscoe gazed at the familiar scenery in silence for the first few minutes of the short ride back to Baraboo. The week had ended much differently than either of them had expected; Marty had officially left the circus to become a theater musician, and Roscoe had gained the confidence to lead a more social life, thanks to his mentor, Clay Edwards.

"I s'pose you're wondering," said Marty after the long silence.

"Wondering about what?" Roscoe asked.

"Why I wanted to go back with you this afternoon instead of leaving on the morning train."

"I hadn't given it much thought, but now that you mention it... no, I wasn't wondering. I knew you had business with your new job this morning, so—"

"That's not why."

Roscoe appeared a little mystified. "Okay... so... why?"

"I... I... I guess 'cause I'm a chicken. I didn't want to get back to town alone and find Jasper waiting for me."

"Hey! If you're afraid of Jasper, that doesn't make you a chicken. Half the people in this town are afraid of Jasper. He's dangerous."

"I know... but I don't want anything to happen now... to ruin my chance to be a theater performer, and Jasper could wreck everything for me."

"So you think I can protect you from him?"

Marty looked at his friend. "Well, two of us together stand a better chance. Me, alone? Hardly."

Marty wasn't a fighter. There was little doubt that he could defend himself against someone like Jasper. He might be adventurous and daring, but he wasn't a fighter.

They both held their breath as the train slowly rolled to a stop at the Baraboo station. It seemed ridiculous to think they would see Jasper and his gang anywhere near, but they scanned the area through the coach windows, just the same. Marty offered to carry Roscoe's satchel while Roscoe grasped the box containing the iced fish.

"We'll go to the store first," Roscoe suggested. "I can get rid of this stuff, and then we'll go to your place."

Marty gave a half-smile. "Thanks, Connor."

The walk from the depot across the river bridge, up the hill to Oak Street and the Mercantile had never seemed so far. Roscoe had imagined his return would feel good after a week's absence, that viewing the brick buildings lined up, the Court House towering above all, the smells and the sounds of the city would be welcoming, but somehow, Marty's circumstances changed all that. Stepping briskly along the sidewalk, keeping one eye on the street ahead and one eye on the sidewalk across the street, a half-block from his father's store Roscoe suddenly reminded himself of the new confidence that Clay Edwards had given him. Scrambling down a busy street in broad daylight scared half out of his wits didn't seem the right way to be managing his self-

77

confidence. He slowed his pace, stretched out his arm to slow Marty's pace as well.

"What?" Marty said. "Do you see him?"

"No," Roscoe replied. "This is crazy. It's broad daylight. There's a hundred Saturday shoppers on this street. We're acting rather foolish. If Jasper did see us, he'd know we're scared, and that's the last thing we want him to think."

"Well," Marty said. "I *am* scared."

"Can't let him see that."

Marty gave one last frantic look up and down the street before they pushed through the Mercantile front door, jangling the little bell above it. Once inside he finally calmed down. A few people mulled around the store; a couple of elderly women greeted Roscoe.

"Hello, Mrs. Anderson. Hello, Mrs. Waldorf," he replied. They were loyal customers of the store for as long as he could remember.

"Hello, Mr. Connor," Marty said with a smile when Roscoe's father greeted them.

"Hello, Mason," came the reply, somewhat surprised to see Roscoe back so early. Long ago, Mr. Connor had picked up on the habit of calling Marty by his last name, just like his son did. "Were you out fishing with Roscoe?"

"Oh... um, no, sir. I... um... just happened to be out at the lake, and we came back together."

Mr. Connor eyed the wooden box that Roscoe carried. "Welcome home, Son. Did you get some good ones?" he asked.

"Sure did." Roscoe lifted the box lid to expose the five Northerns.

"Well, that'll make a couple of fine suppers. Better get them into the icebox upstairs."

"Okay, Pop, and then I'm going with Mason over to his house, and then I've got some things to do."

"What things?"

"Shopping... it's time for some new summer clothes."

Mr. Connor studied Marty's attire. "Aren't those your clothes that Mason's wearing?"

"Oh... yeah."

"Why is he wearing your clothes?"

"Well, Mason ended up at the lake kinda unexpected... he didn't have any extra clothes along, so he borrowed some of mine."

Mr. Connor sensed that his son and Marty were trying to hide something, obviously on edge about something they weren't eager to divulge. "Okay... you boys want to explain what's going on?"

The boys squirmed. "Well, Pop," Roscoe said. "Marty had a little confrontation with Jasper a few days ago... that's why he ended up at the lake... to get away. He stayed with me at the hotel until things cooled down."

"Jasper? What kind of confrontation? Did he hurt you?"

"No," Marty said. "He didn't get the chance. A new friend of ours kinda saved me."

"So, what was the confrontation about?"

"I sorta suggested to Jasper that he could get a

job as a clown in the circus... but I was just trying to be helpful. He didn't take too kindly to it, though."

Mr. Connor's face beamed with delight, and then he laughed. "A clown! How entertaining! I'll bet he'd make a charming clown!"

"But he was serious, Mr. Connor. He wanted to kill me!"

"And that's why I'm walking with him to his house," Roscoe added.

"I wouldn't worry too much, Mason. He's probably already forgotten about it."

ELEVEN

"What a relief!" Eleanor Mason said to Marty on the front porch steps. "I thought you'd run off with those circus people again without even saying good-bye."

"Ma... you know I wouldn't do that."

"So, where have you been?"

"Well, for starters, Toby broke his arm, and I stayed at his house and helped his mom with chores."

"Good heavens! How'd he break his arm?"

Marty chuckled. "Fell out of a tree."

"What was he doing in a tree?"

"Trying to get their cat down... but he should've just left her, 'cause she eventually came down on her own."

"Is he gonna be alright?"

"He'll be fine... he just won't be playing the trombone for a while."

"Here it is Saturday! Roscoe Connor came by last Monday looking for you." She locked her arm around his and together they stepped through the front door of their modest little house.

"Yeah, I know... he found me, and I've been out at the lake with him since then."

Eleanor looked Marty up and down. "Whose clothes are you wearing? They certainly aren't yours."

"No, Ma. They're Connor's. I borrowed them."

"Aren't the clothes I make for you good enough anymore?"

"Yeah, Ma... they're just fine. But my favorite yellow shirt and brown trousers got dirty, so I borrowed some clothes from Connor."

"Well, where are the dirty clothes? I'll have to wash them."

"I guess I forgot to get them out of Connor's satchel when we came back."

"Just like you... oh, well. I'll get them from his mother Tuesday after work. But right now I need you to help me move the sofa."

Eleanor Mason spent most of her week as a seamstress in a shop downtown. Saturday and Monday were her days off, and the shop wasn't open on Sunday, so she made the most of the three days with all the chores at home. This weekend had been designated for spring cleaning.

"I'm not going back to the circus this year," Marty said as they shoved the heavy Victorian sofa across the sitting room.

Eleanor stood upright, her eyes wide, not sure if she should be happy because her baby was not running away with the circus again, or upset because he had apparently quit his job. "Well... what *are* you going to do?"

"I have a new job as a theater pianist. I joined up with a theater troupe this week at the lake."

"What theater troupe?"

"They're new here... you wouldn't know them?"

"But you were doing so well with the Ringlings."

"I know, Ma... but I don't want to chase all over the country living in a train car for the next six months." Marty took his mother's hand and they sat on the displaced sofa. "I met these people at the Cliff House. I gave some auditions... and they like me. Mr. Bordeaux wants me to come back on Monday to start rehearsals."

"You mean... you'll be living at home?"

"Some of the time. I guess we'll be traveling some, too, but staying in hotels with regular beds, and not in some stinky old train car bunk."

"Sounds like vaudeville, and it sounds like your mind is made up."

"It's what I wanna do, Ma. It's my chance to become a real performer."

Eleanor grinned. "Well, then... we'll have to make you some new clothes! Theodore at the shop will fit you with a new suit, and—"

"Ma! They have a wardrobe. They'll dress me the way *they* want me dressed."

"Well, you'll still need some nice traveling clothes." There was no stopping Eleanor Mason when it came to making new clothes for her only son. He was going to get them whether he wanted them or not.

Safe at his mother's house—the only place he'd ever known as home—Marty tried to put the Jasper incident out of his thoughts. Now he needed to focus on a grander life; yes, even grander than the circus. Instead of stuffing himself into a hot, uncomfortable band uniform for ten hours a day, he'd be donned in silk shirts and tuxedos. He would be living a normal life, spending his time with people he enjoyed being with. Oh, it would be a lot of hard work, too, practicing and preparing for shows. But he was up to it, ready and eager to meet the challenge.

Sitting there on the back porch steps, Marty realized that he had nearly forgotten the beauty when the earth emerged and once again faced the spring sun. Tiny leaves of green sprouted from the gray branches of the skeleton trees, birds trilled their spring songs, and all the spring scents took to the air. He just sat there, breathing it all in until his mother called him to supper.

That night he climbed the dark stairway to his attic bedroom, but somehow, now it didn't seem so lonely. His life seemed changed with the season; he felt an odd sense of freedom that could take him anywhere he wanted to go.

His bedroom window that had been stuck closed

all winter opened freely allowing the fresh spring air to flow in. The wintery dryness of his little room drifted away as the tantalizing breeze whipped across his bed and then danced on to the other rooms. He undressed and lay on his bed, the coolness washing over him until he settled into a restful sleep.

Marty awoke the next morning sweating under a heap of quilts and blankets that had protected him from the cold night air freely pouring in through the open window. He couldn't remember getting under the blankets; now they were smothering him. He threw them aside and abruptly sat up, rubbing the sleep from his eyes. He yawned and stretched the stiffness from his legs; the chilly morning air shocked him fully awake. He planted both feet on the cold floor, stood, and then strode contentedly to the open window. Gradually, the memories of yesterday crept into his thoughts as he felt the warmth of the sunlight on his face. It was going to be a great summer.

TWELVE

"**M**A! I can only find one white shirt. Where's my other white shirt?" Marty's Monday morning anxiety was building; he wanted to be ready to leave in a half-hour, giving him plenty of time to visit with Roscoe at the store before he boarded the train to the lake. He'd promised that he would.

"Why do you need *two* white shirts?" Eleanor replied from the bottom of the stairway.

"'Cause I'm gonna be staying out there for a few days. I need an extra shirt."

"Can't you take something else? Your other white shirt is down at the shop... I was mending a seam and I forgot to bring it home. Take the blue one."

Marty closed his eyes and shook his head, but then he admitted to himself that he shouldn't be taking out his frustrations on his mother; after all, she had his best interests at heart. A blue shirt was better than no shirt. He carefully folded it and put it in his satchel. One last inspection in the mirror: white shirt, black bowtie, charcoal gray coat and trousers—even though they weren't the most fashionable—shined shoes. He was ready to meet the day!

He could smell the bacon frying downstairs, and when he reached the kitchen after putting his satchel by the front door, a plate with the bacon, two hard-boiled eggs and a glass of milk were already on the table waiting for him.

"My, my, look at you," Eleanor said. "Are you preaching or playing the piano?"

"I just want to look good," Marty replied. "The fellows I will be rehearsing with always look good... especially Clay. He always looks like he just stepped out of a custom tailor shop."

"And so will you when Theodore finishes your new suit. What color would you prefer? Black, blue, or gray?"

"Burgundy," Marty said. "I need to be..." He hesitated, searching for the right word.

"Different?" Eleanor suggested.

"Yeah... different," Marty agreed. He sat down to devour the bacon and eggs. "And tell Theodore I will be in for the final fitting when I come back from the lake."

"Final fitting! He's made suits for you before...

he has your measurements."

"But this one has to fit perfect. Tell him I'll pay extra."

"But I can pay for—"

"No, you can't. I'll pay for the new suit myself. You can make some fancy shirts to go with it. Okay?"

Marty finished the bacon and eggs, got up from the table and started for the front door with Eleanor right on his heels. "Thanks for the breakfast, Ma. I'm gonna stop and see Connor before I catch the train to the lake."

"When will you be back?" She gave Marty a motherly kiss on his cheek.

"Don't know... maybe Thursday or Friday." He picked up the satchel, donned his cap from the hall tree, and headed out the door. At the bottom of the porch steps he turned and blew her a kiss. "Love ya, Ma."

It had been a week since Jasper Blackburn had made his assault; Marty hoped that Mr. Connor was right in assuming that he'd forgotten by now. But it was difficult not to think about the possible threat waiting around any corner, amidst any shadow, behind any tree. He hadn't mentioned a word of this to his mother because he didn't want her to worry; in his absence, he hoped the bully wouldn't bother her.

He was nearly half-way to Oak Street when he heard the horses and a buckboard coming up on him from behind. He veered off to the side of the road to give the team a wide berth. But as the wagon was even with him, it slowed down and kept pace with Marty's step.

"Hey! Mason!" a voice called to him.

Marty looked up at the driver and his passenger aboard the wagon. "Hey, Dobbs. What you doin' here?"

"Been waitin' for ya."

"Why?"

"Thought y' might like t' go for a little ride with me 'n Frank."

"Can't. I'm going to see my friend, Connor, 'n then I gotta catch a train."

"Well, then... hop on. I'll give y' a ride there."

"It's just down to Oak Street."

Dobbs reined the horses to the right and then to a stop, cutting off Marty's path. Dobbs and Frank were on the ground almost instantly, one on either side of Marty. With firm grips, they hoisted him up on the buckboard seat, and then sat themselves again, sandwiching Marty between them. Dobbs slapped the reins on the horses' backs, and in a flurry they rode off toward the river.

THIRTEEN

I t was decided; *Oliver Twist* had been such an overwhelming success the previous season in Montana; Simon couldn't think of any good reason not to keep it as their opening play here in Wisconsin. Less time would be involved than preparing for a new production. They had all the props, scenery backdrops, and costumes. Only the new piano man needed to learn the music and his cues. Of course, there would still be all the vaudeville acts, too—the songs, comedy, dance routines—that filled in on the nights they didn't perform a play.

"I hate waiting for trains," Christian told Clay. "Especially when they're late."

Clay nonchalantly gazed up and down the tracks. The train was late, but only by fifteen minutes, so far.

"If I remember correctly," he said, "Y'all used to spend a lot of time waiting for trains to arrive at Silver Spring."

"That was different."

"How?"

"Then it was my job... getting people to the hotel."

"Well, then," Clay replied. "This isn't any different; y'all are here to get Marty Mason to the hotel. It's just not the same hotel."

Clay's attempt didn't ease Christian's impatience. He had spent all weekend rearranging and cleaning the piano room so they had some space for rehearsals, and he was anxious to get started. Marty's arrival would put everything in motion.

The whistle echoing among the Baraboo Hills gave Christian a little relief; finally, the train was arriving, and with it their new piano man. In his mind, Christian could hear the applauding audiences; he could smell the grease paint; he could feel the heat from the footlights.

The engine chuffed by with its usual clouds of smoke and steam nearly smothering everything in its wake. When the coaches finally came to rest, the conductor stepped off onto the platform, ushering a number of passengers from the train while porters scrambled about with luggage. Christian paced back and forth on the platform in a space no bigger than a closet. He hadn't seen Marty.

The conductor was calling all aboard, but Marty still hadn't stepped out of the coach.

"Are y'all sure this is the right train?" Clay asked.

"Monday... first afternoon train," Christian replied. "Yeah, I'm sure this is the right train."

"Maybe he just got mixed up on the time... or maybe he just forgot."

"Anxious as he was, I don't think he forgot."

"What'll we tell Simon?"

"I don't know. Let's check the telegraph office... see if there's any message from him."

There was just enough room for them to get on the little steamboat back to the Cliff House. It might have been quicker to walk, but now there didn't seem to be any reason to hurry. When they arrived at the north end of the lake, they didn't waste any time getting to the Cliff House telegraph office; the agent checked all the undelivered incoming messages he had received that day. "Sorry boys... there's nothing from a Marty Mason."

"Will you let us know right away if anything comes in?"

The operator nodded and then abruptly directed his attention to the clackety-clack-clack of the telegraph key. Christian and Clay left.

Simon eyed the two young actors as they entered the room that had become a rehearsal stage. He kept watching the doorway, expecting Marty. "So where's our new piano man?"

"Marty wasn't on this train," Christian replied. "Maybe the next one."

But Marty wasn't on the next train, either, and for two more days, rehearsals went on with Clyde providing the musical effects on violin as best he could. By Wednesday, everyone was getting impatient; Simon was on edge; good, talented pianists were hard to find. "Christian... why isn't our piano man here? How can we expect the Silver Spring Players to get a show ready without our piano man?"

"We can't, Simon."

"I expected Mr. Mason to be more dependable than this," Simon uttered.

"And as well as I got to know him last week, I'm sure he is."

"But we agreed that he would start rehearsing with us on Monday. In case you haven't noticed, it is now Wednesday."

"Yes, Simon," Christian said. "I'm getting worried that something bad has happened to him."

"What could have possibly happened?" Simon asked. "He was only going to his home in Baraboo."

"Well," Christian hesitated. "Marty's been known to get himself into compromising situations."

"Oh?"

"Yes... that's how we actually met him."

"I thought his friend, Roscoe introduced you."

"He did, but when we went to Baraboo to find him, he was... um..."

Clay stepped in. "Marty was engaged in a personal dispute that was about to become rather unfavorable to his well-being."

Simon stared questioningly.

"You see," Christian tried again. "There was this gang of roughnecks..."

"Oh, great!" Simon blurted. "We've signed on a

ruffian—"

"On the contrary," Clay corrected him. "The roughnecks Christian is talking about... well... there was five of 'em... they intended to offer Marty a little unfriendly guidance down to the ground. He was at an unfair advantage... so me 'n Christian 'n Roscoe sorta stepped in with a little assistance."

Simon quickly evaluated Clay's explanation that clearly described the beginnings of a brawl. "Well that's just what we need... my star performers getting involved in a public display of violence in the street!"

"Oh! No!" Christian said. "It wasn't public at all... we were in an alley where nobody saw us."

"Violence, just the same," Simon said.

By this time, Charlotte, Victor, Clyde, and Vivian had gathered around, quite amused with the developing account.

"Contrary to your assumption," Clay explained, "We did not engage in any violent acts. Our intervention caused a far more suitable outcome."

"But you two aren't much bigger than knee-high to a bumblebee... how could you dare stand up to a gang like that?"

Clay extended his right arm toward Simon and patted the cuff of his coat sleeve with his left hand. "My shiny little friend persuaded them to pursue other endeavors."

Simon and the others were acquainted with the actor's personal background, and quite aware of his habitual practice to conceal a derringer in his coat sleeve. "Clay!" Simon exclaimed. "You attacked them with a gun?"

"Not attacked... defended," Clay rebutted. "And in a quiet and dignified manner."

"That's when we brought Marty here on the train," Christian added. "We had to get him out of town for a while... for his own safety."

Simon stared some more, shocked, stern. "I thought we left such vicious conduct back in Montana."

"Doesn't matter if y'all are in Montana or Wisconsin," Clay offered in his calm Southern drawl. "If a man is fixin' to bash your head in with a lead pipe, then I'd think y'all would have the right to defend yourself."

Now their audience—the rest of the troupe—sided with Clay; Clyde put a hand on Clay's shoulder. "I agree," he confided. "You did the right thing."

"Bully for you!" Victor chimed in.

"We're so lucky to have you here with us," Vivian Moon cooed. "That was brave and honorable."

Simon had no choice but to concede; his unfavorable view of the alley incident seemed to be the unpopular one among the group. But nevertheless, he was still upset with the premature loss of the new piano player.

Charlotte Van Horne, who had clearly thrown numerous lustful glances in Marty's direction the night of the welcoming dinner party, openly expressed her conjecture: "So, when are you two heroes gonna go find him and bring him back here *again?"*

Christian and Clay exchanged brief but thoughtful glimpses.

"Perhaps we should," Clay said.

"We could take the next train," Christian added. He had been considering that option all morning.

"Then go," Simon demanded. "Find Marty... or *another* piano man. Just bring somebody back here who can play our music."

FOURTEEN

C lay and Christian stepped off the train at the Baraboo station. They had no baggage, as they didn't intend to stay any longer than it required locating Marty, and if time allowed a cordial visit with Roscoe at the Mercantile. Roscoe had taken them to Marty's house once before; they could find it again, hopeful that the search would end there, and they could all get on the next train back to the lake.

"D'ya think this will turn into another rescue mission?" Christian asked as they crossed the bridge over the Baraboo River.

"Well, if it does, I packed a little extra ammunition."

"And I couldn't help notice... by the bulge under

your coat... you also packed the forty-five."

"I did. Y'all never know these days."

They walked along Water Street to where they turned away from the river and up the hill towards the neighborhood where Marty and his mother lived. At the top of the hill, Clay shaded his eyes from the bright sun. "Okay... which one is it? I know we're close."

Christian pointed. "That one. Down towards the end of the block. The one with the two maples in the front yard."

They were just about to knock on the front door when a voice called to them from the next yard. "Ain't nobody home at the Mason's."

Christian looked toward the woman who had her hands full with fallen twigs and leaves. "We're friends of Marty's," he responded. "Have you seen him?"

"Not since the weekend," the woman said.

"How 'bout Marty's mum?"

"Eleanor's a seamstress at the tailor shop over on Oak Street."

"Thank y'all, Ma'am," said Clay. He tipped his hat. "We'll talk to her there."

They knew Oak Street; it was on Oak Street where Connor's Mercantile occupied space in the middle of a block—the block they had avoided when searching for Marty the first time. But now there was no need to skirt around it, and they wanted to stop in for a visit with Roscoe, anyway.

Although they had not seen it before, large red

and white letters spelling the name on the big plate glass windows made it quite easy to find. Across the street and down a few doors they spotted a tailor shop, perhaps the one where Mrs. Mason worked. "Let's go there first," suggested Christian.

"Good idea," Clay replied. "I could use a new suit." He stood back a step or two from Christian and examined his friend's attire. "And so could y'all."

"Yeah, well, we don't have time for that right now."

"We can look, can't we?"

Just inside the front door, a big green parrot on a high perch squawked a greeting: "NEW SUIT! NEW SUIT!" A few seconds later, from a doorway draped with only a curtain a bald-headed man emerged, shirt sleeves rolled up to the elbows and a bright yellow tape measure dangled around his neck. "Aaaaaa! Gentlemen... welcome. I am Theodore Baskin, proprietor."

Clay scanned the room, its walls lined with dozens of bolts of fabric of all colors and textures. Above them on one side of the studio hung artists' renderings of men, young and old, clad in various fashionable suits, and on the other side, the wall was adorned with pictures of women in elegant gowns and dresses.

Theodore continued his pitch: "As you can see, we have a wide assortment of only the finest fabrics... and a good variety of colors and patterns. Would you be looking for everyday or formal apparel?"

Clay was captivated by the quality surrounding him. "We both need new suits," he said as he gazed at the rolls of fine cloth.

"But not today," Christian interrupted. "Actually, we're looking for someone."

"NEW SUIT! NEW SUIT!" the bird squawked again.

Theodore turned to the parrot. "Napoleon... that's quite enough!" Then he turned to Christian again. "And who would you be looking for?"

"Is this where Eleanor Mason works?"

"It is."

"Could we please talk to her? It's kinda important."

When Christian noticed the woman that came from behind the curtain covering the work room doorway, he immediately recognized her as the woman he had seen at the Mason's house more than a week ago.

"I heard someone mention my name," she said.

"These gentlemen are here to see you, Ellie," Theodore said.

"Mrs. Mason," Christian said. "I don't know if you remember us. Roscoe brought us to your house Monday before last... we were looking for Marty."

"Yes..." she said, showing a little reluctance. "I remember your faces, but I don't believe we were properly introduced."

"Oh, yes... well, I'm Christian Parker, and this is Clay Edwards."

Clay took Eleanor's hand, bowed from the waist and kissed her fingers. "Pleased to meet you,

Ma'am," he said in his gentlemanly southern intonation.

Eleanor's face beamed with pleasure. She wasn't used to such behavior. "What is it that I can do for you gentlemen?"

"Clay and I are part of the theater troupe staying out at the Cliff House..."

"Oh, yes," Eleanor said. "Marty was so thrilled to join your group. He talked about you all weekend."

"He was s'posed to come out on the train to start rehearsing with us on Monday," Clay explained.

"Yes, he packed a suitcase and left our house Monday just before noon... said that he'd be at the lake for a few days."

"Well..." Christian hesitated. "He wasn't on that train or any train since."

Eleanor's beaming smile faded. "You mean... he's not..."

"No, he's not with us at the hotel. We thought we should come here to see if he'd changed his mind."

Now Eleanor's faded smile gradually melted into a frown. "I doubt that he would have changed his mind. Once he decides to do something, there's no changing him... like the circus last year. I couldn't talk him out of that for all the coconuts in Brazil."

"Are y'all sure he left on the noon train?" Clay asked.

Eleanor thought a moment. "Well... he said... he said he would... but..."

"But what, Mrs. Mason?"

"I think he said he was going to stop in and see

Connor before he boarded the train... yes... I'm sure of that."

"Okay... we'll check with him next."

"Please," Eleanor begged. "Do let me know what you find out."

"Don't worry, Ma'am. We'll find Marty."

As they headed for the door, Theodore called out to them: "When you see Marty, tell him I have his new suit ready for the final fitting."

Napoleon got in the last word: "NEW SUIT. NEW SUIT."

FIFTEEN

The little bell jangled profoundly as Christian pushed open the front door of the Mercantile. It startled him just slightly as he paused and stared up at the bell. Clay pushed him inside and closed the door behind them. The bell jangled some more. They were standing in the spacious store amidst an array of goods varying from pots and pans to picture frames and everything else imaginable. It was no wonder that the store was busy with customers browsing about and considering their choices for purchase.

A young man whom Christian barely recognized came from behind a counter to greet them. Roscoe beamed a broad smile when he saw them, glad that his new friends from the lake had come to pay him a visit.

Christian stared at Roscoe for a few moments; he had always seen him dressed in casual and somewhat drab clothing, appropriate for informal outdoor activities such as fishing and hiking in the woods. But today, he was gazing at a gentleman in garments that reminded him of a larger version of Clay! The bold black coat, open in front to reveal the matching vest, fit like it was custom-tailored, crisp white shirt and black string tie, shined boots—Christian couldn't help but wonder if there was a derringer up his sleeve, too.

"Well..." Clay said as he looked the store clerk up and down. "So this is the Roscoe when he's not out fishing. He certainly has a fine taste in clothes... don't y'all think so, Christian?"

"I'm so glad you're here," said Roscoe. His face reddened just a little knowing his visitors noticed his new suit. "What brings you two into Baraboo?"

"We came to see y'all... of course," Clay smiled. He was definitely impressed by Roscoe's appearance.

"And to find Marty Mason," Christian added. "But it's really good to see you again, too."

Roscoe gave Christian a curious gaze. "Lookin' for Mason?"

Just then, another man richly attired in a dark green suit joined them.

"Hey, Pop," Roscoe said. "I want you to meet my friends from the lake. This is Clay Edwards and Christian Parker."

Mr. Connor smoothed his mustache with his fingertips and then removed his wire-rimmed reading spectacles, peering at the two. "I'm Jacob Connor, Roscoe's father," he said as he offered his firm handshake. "I've heard much about you from my son, Mr. Edwards, and I can now see that you've had a bit more influence on him than I first suspected."

"I hope y'all don't mean that in a bad way, sir," Clay said.

"Not at all. Roscoe seems to have gained a little fortitude since his week at the lake."

"Yeah, well, a week of fishing could do that."

"He said he learned from *you*, Mr. Edwards. And now I see how his altered preference in garments has come about."

Clay quickly glanced down at his own suit, and then briefly scanned Roscoe's, confirming the remarkable resemblance. "Oh, well, I really didn't mean to suggest that he should—"

"Tut-tut," said Mr. Connor. "You should be flattered. Now, if you will kindly excuse me, I think those ladies over there by the sewing notions may need some assistance. I'll leave you three gents to continue your conversation."

Clay tipped his hat, nodded, and watched Mr. Connor stroll away. "Your father is certainly an honorable man," he said to Roscoe.

"Sure he is..." Roscoe said in a low tone. "...now that he thinks I'm dressed more appropriately... for him and his store. I just wish he'd understand that I don't really want to be here. I want to go out and see the world."

"And just how d' y'all propose to do that?"

"Well, I figure you will be moving on someday, and when you do, maybe I'll go with you."

"Us? Move on?"

"Sure. All entertainers move on... sooner or later."

It was true; neither Clay nor Christian intended to stay here in Wisconsin for the rest of their lives. Although they felt a certain degree of loyalty and gratitude to Simon Bordeaux, and intended to stay with him—at least for the rest of this season —they both had bigger dreams. Christian had visions of performing on the stages of the magnificent theaters in New York; and Clay... well... he wasn't sure that he would continue his career as an actor, but he knew that he wanted to see London, Paris, Madrid, Rome, and maybe Hong Kong.

Roscoe saw that distant look in Christian's and Clay's eyes at the mention of a common trait in show people. "It's true, ain't it?" Roscoe said. "Now, what's this about you lookin' for Mason? I thought he was with you at the lake already."

"Yeah," Clay said. "He was s'posed to come on the first afternoon train on Monday... but he never showed up."

"We talked to his mum over at the tailor shop... said he packed a bag and left Monday before noon... that he was coming to see you first."

"Yeah," Roscoe said. "I was plenty pissed off when he didn't come like he promised. I picked up this new suit from the tailor that morning... just in time so Mason could see it."

"And a splendid suit it is," Clay affirmed. He ran his fingers along the edge of the lapel, and then gently grasped Roscoe's wrist, feeling and patting the sleeve from the cuff to the elbow.

"What are you doing?" Roscoe asked.

"Just checking to see if Theodore installed a pocket for some light artillery."

"No... but he said he would..."

Clay grinned.

"Any idea where Marty went?" Christian pleaded.

Roscoe contemplated for just a moment. "No... and I don't care... now that he's run out on *you*, and never told *me* where he was going."

"But maybe he never left town," Clay said. "Maybe he's still here. How 'bout other friends... maybe he's with them."

"Me and Mason don't have many friends."

"Well, Connor, would y'all at least help us look for him? Y'all know this town better than us."

It suddenly occurred to Roscoe that Clay had just called him *Connor*, like Mason always did. Even though he was still upset about his best friend brushing him off, he felt a little distress, too. "I have to work," he said, trying to hide his uneasiness.

"But aren't y'all just a little concerned about Mason?"

Roscoe started to cave in. "Well, I can ask Pop if I can leave for a while."

Mr. Connor didn't see the urgency in Mason's desertion. "You know, Roscoe, he's vanished before...

and he always turns up again, just like a bad penny."

"He's not a bad penny, Pop."

"He ran off last summer to join the circus... remember?"

"But he didn't leave then without saying goodbye."

"He'll turn up, Roscoe."

"But, Pop. Clay and Christian are part of a theater group, and Mason's s'posed to be practicing with them... they're depending on him."

"Mason will eventually turn up," Mr. Connor insisted. "Now, there's someone at the cash register waiting to pay. Go take care of her and stop worrying about Mason."

Roscoe obeyed his father's orders and returned to the counter. He dispatched a frown to Clay and Christian. They understood his message, waved, and headed to the door.

"We'll just have to look around on our own," Christian suggested. "He's gotta be here somewhere."

"Let's try the circus grounds," Clay said. "Maybe a chance..."

SIXTEEN

C hristian shuddered to think that Marty might have changed his mind and had returned to the circus. But the only way to know for sure was to go there and ask a few questions. They crossed the river bridge again and turned toward the circus lot along the river with no idea of who they should approach, but somebody would certainly guide them in the right direction. As they got closer, they could hear brassy music that was definitely being produced by a Big Top band.

"Hear that?" Christian said. "The band is here somewhere practicing."

"Yeah," Clay replied. "We find that band and we prob'ly find Marty."

"As much as I want to find Marty, I hope we *don't* find him *there*."

They found the band on a large wooden platform

under an open tent. The musicians sat on wooden chairs in a semi-circle around the band leader at a podium, feverishly waving his arms in direction as the band played a lively Sousa march.

"He certainly isn't lacking in enthusiasm, is he?" Clay commented.

Christian agreed, but kept inching around the tent, until he spotted a piano partially hidden from his view by a bass drum and a tuba. When he finally got in position to clearly see the pianist, he let out a sigh of relief. It *wasn't* Marty.

When the march ended, the band leader noticed Christian attempting to get the attention of one of the drummers in the back row. "Either speak up so we can hear you, or kindly stop interrupting our practice."

"I'm sorry," Christian spoke up. "We're looking for Marty Mason."

"Mr. Mason isn't with us this year."

"I know that... but we were wondering if anyone here might have seen him recently?"

Christian could tell by the murmurs and whispers circulating among the musicians that nearly everyone there probably knew Marty, and he hoped for something positive.

A trumpet player spoke up: "You might try Toby Atwood's house."

"Who's Toby Atwood?"

"He's a trombone player... but he's out with a broken arm. Toby and Marty chummed a lot."

"And where do we find Toby Atwood's house?"

"It's the brown house behind the big white church... over there on the hill." The trumpet player pointed across the river.

"Okay... thank you," said Christian. He nodded and waved to the conductor. "Thank you," he said again.

The conductor rapped his baton on the podium a few times to get the attention of his band again. "Okay... let's do that one again... and this time we'll slow the tempo..."

Christian and Clay were already on their way back to the bridge. "D'ya think we'll find this Toby Atwood?" Christian asked.

"Don't know. Did Marty every mention him to y'all?"

"Not that I remember."

As they hustled along the river after they had crossed the bridge, they could still hear the circus band playing the same tune with a few variations from the first time they heard it. Clay noticed something that didn't look quite natural among some weeds and bushes still clinging to their brown leaves from last fall.

"What is it?" Christian asked when Clay detoured to the dry foliage.

"Looks like... maybe..." Clay mumbled as he dug his way through the dry branches and weeds. He pulled up a brown canvas satchel, noticing by its weight and firmness that it contained something... perhaps clothes. "It hasn't been here long," he said. "It's too clean and dry to have been here a long time." Then, after flipping it over to examine all sides he turned to Christian with a somber stare.

"What's wrong?" Christian asked.

Clay stepped out of the bushes to where Christian was standing and held the satchel so he could see the stenciled name on the bag next to the handle.

Christian read the name: "M. Mason. My God... this is Marty's!"

"Yeah... but how'd it get in those bushes? And why?"

Christian thought a long moment. "There has to be a good explanation for this." He thought some more. "Perhaps Toby Atwood has the answer."

They climbed the hill, found the little brown house behind the church and when they knocked, a woman opened the door.

"What're ya peddling?" she said before the young men could even say hello. "Whatever it is, I don't want any."

"Oh, we're not peddling anything, Ma'am," Clay charmed. "We're looking for Toby Atwood. Are we at the right house?"

The woman wiped her hands on her apron, all the while her eyes fixed on the two Dandies in their attractive suits. "What ya want with Toby? He in some kinda trouble?"

"Oh, no, Ma'am. We have a mutual friend... Marty Mason... and Marty's gone missing... wondered if Toby knows of his whereabouts."

"I ain't seen hide nor hair of Marty for over a week," the woman said. Her words were sharp.

"But if we could talk to Toby..."

Another voice sounded from inside the house. "It's okay, Ma, I'll talk to 'em." A young man appeared behind the woman; his right arm bent in a cast and supported by a sling.

"Are y'all Toby?" Clay asked.

"Yeah... who are you?"

"I'm Clay Edwards... and this is Christian Parker. We're friends of Marty's."

Toby stepped out of the shadows, now crowding his mother out of the doorway. "Go back to your baking, Ma," he said. "I'll handle this."

Mrs. Atwood backed away, and then disappeared into the interior of the house.

"Friends of Marty's," Toby said with certain suspicion in his words. "Never saw you around before."

"No, y'all prob'ly haven't. We just met Marty a week ago Monday."

"Why did ya come here looking for me?"

"A trumpet player in the circus band told us y'all might know where to find Marty."

"When did you last see him?" Christian asked.

"Well, let's see..." Toby scratched his head with his left hand. "Broke my arm Friday. Mason came over, stayed here Saturday and Sunday, and then when we woke up Monday morning, he said he had to go up town, but he didn't go right away."

"And y'all haven't seen him since?"

Toby shook his head thoughtfully. "No... said he was coming back, but I never saw him all last week."

"Because he was with us at the lake all last week."

"The lake! What was he doin' there? He should've been at band practice."

"Yes... well... Marty's not in the circus band anymore," Christian explained. "He joined our theater troupe. He's our piano man now."

Toby shook his head in a slow, indecisive manner. "Well, I guess I'm not in the band anymore, either."

"Why do y'all say that?"

"Kinda hard to play the trombone with your right arm in a cast."

"But your arm will heal."

"Doc says I'll have this cast for eight weeks... the circus train will be a thousand miles from here by then."

"I'm sorry," Clay consoled.

"It's okay... there's always next year."

"What do y'all know about a fellow named Jasper?"

"Jasper Blackburn? Yeah, I know him. He's not someone you'd want to marry your sister. Why do you ask?"

"Did y'all know that Mason and Jasper had a little confrontation after he left here?"

"No, I didn't," Toby said. "But it doesn't surprise me."

"Oh? Why?"

"They've been enemies for as long as I can remember."

The jangling door bell at the Mercantile didn't startle Christian and Clay this time, but the urgency in their arrival made Roscoe take notice. By the expression on Christian's face, he sensed that something had gone wrong. "Hi Clay," he said. "Did you find Mason?"

"No, but we had a good chat with his friend, Toby Atwood."

"Toby! You talked to Toby? I heard he broke his arm. Did he know anything about Mason?"

"Marty had been there... just before we rescued him in the alley, but Toby hasn't seen him since. And we found this... in some bushes down by the river." Clay held up the brown canvas satchel, turned so Roscoe could see the name.

Roscoe stared at the bag. "That's Mason's all right. Did you open it?"

"No, not yet."

They put the satchel on a counter. Roscoe undid the buckles, flipped back the top, and then pulled out a blue coat and trousers, blue shirt, ties, socks. "These are definitely his clothes. Looks like he planned to stay at the lake for a while."

"But why would he toss it in the bushes?" Christian asked.

"And that isn't even on his way to the depot," Clay added, "unless he was going to see Toby again before he left."

"I guess that's possible," Roscoe admitted. "They did chum together a lot after Mason joined the circus band."

"Well, he never made it back to Toby's. Y'all got any other ideas where he might've gone?"

117

"What's this all about?" Mr. Connor asked when he eyed the open satchel and Marty's clothes on the counter.

"Mason's disappeared, Pop... I mean... *really* disappeared. They found his bag down by the river in some weeds. It just don't seem right... d' ya think?"

"Hello, gentlemen," Mr. Connor greeted Christian and Clay. "Nice to see you again," and then he contemplated for a long moment. "You know... Mason's been known to run off for a spell now and then."

"Yeah, I know... but why would he leave his clothes behind in some weeds? It just don't make any sense."

"Tell ya what, Son... why don't you go with these gentlemen and ask around town... see if anybody knows of Mason's whereabouts."

When Christian and Clay returned to the Cliff House late that night, they were too tired to do anything but to get to their room and go to bed. Their search for Marty with Roscoe guiding them for four hours had rendered no results. No one they talked to had seen Marty for over a week. It was discouraging to say the least.

Next morning at breakfast, Simon found them in the hotel dining hall.

"By the long faces I would guess that you didn't locate our missing piano player?"

"Um... we found a trail," Christian started to explain.

Simon stared with expectation.

Then Clay continued. "We found where he'd been and who he'd been with... a week ago... but..."

"But what? Where is he now?"

"We don't know for sure." Clay stared into the tablecloth. "We sorta lost him."

"Well," Simon said. "I'm sure he'll turn up soon."

"We're going back into town today," Christian added. "To look some more."

A waitress brought Simon's plate of pancakes.

Simon lowered his voice and leaned in. "I have something important to tell you. I haven't told the others yet."

Christian and Clay leaned in, too, eyes wide.

"I've located a building for our new theater."

"Simon! That's great! Where is it?"

"It's an old storefront on Third Street. I'm going to the bank on Friday to sign the papers. We can take possession next week."

"Friday... that's tomorrow," Christian said. Then he turned to Clay. "We've gotta find Marty."

"It'll be several weeks until the carpenters have the place ready to use," Simon explained. "But I do wish you'd get our piano man back here for rehearsals. And then, perhaps, we should put him on a leash."

"We'll make this next trip to town a crusade," Christian vowed.

Clay laughed. "Does that mean we have to wear armor?"

Christian gave a hardly noticeable wink. "No... just the usual hardware."

SEVENTEEN

"**W**e should make another visit to Toby Atwood," Clay suggested as they walked from the Baraboo station. "I think he knows more than he told us."

"What makes you think so?"

"Because he didn't hesitate when he said that Marty and Jasper had been enemies for as long as he could remember."

"Yeah? So?"

"So, that means he knows more about what's between those two. And of all the people we heard Roscoe talk to, did y'all hear anyone mention any other enemies that Marty might have?"

Christian thought a moment. "No, I guess you're right about that."

"So, we need to talk to Toby again."

"Okay... but let's go see Roscoe first. Maybe he's

heard something... or at least we can let him know we're here. Maybe he'll go with us."

The walk to Oak Street was most pleasant; there were kids and birds and pretty ladies in their new spring dresses fussing about in their gardens of budding flowers. The smell and the feel of summertime filled the day.

For Clay and Christian, a new opera house would soon be a part of their lives. It didn't seem right that they should be wasting precious time hunting for a missing piano player; they should be preparing for the shows. But Marty had become a good friend, too, and if he had found trouble, they should help.

As usual, they found Roscoe Connor at the Mercantile strutting among the customers in his spiffy new suit. The jangling bell averted his attention to the door.

"Clay. Christian. Good to see you again. Any new developments?" He shook their hands.

"No, but we thought we would pay Toby Atwood another visit. Can y'all join us?"

"I'd like to, but I'm afraid I'm stuck here for a time while Pop tends to a few business errands."

"Well, okay... we don't want to keep y'all from your customers. We'll see y'all later, then."

Mrs. Atwood said nothing when she opened the door and discovered Clay and Christian standing on the porch. Leaving the door wide open, she disappeared into another room, and then they heard her call Toby's name. A few seconds later, Toby was there at the door, stepped out onto the porch and closed the door behind him.

"Hi, Toby."

"What are you doing back here again?"

"Wanted to see if y'all might've heard from Mason..."

"No, I ain't heard from him."

"Okay... so what is it with Mason and Jasper? What's their feud about?"

"Started over a girl. But that's a long time ago."

"Who won the girl?"

"Neither... she moved away... to Reedsburg."

"Where's Reedsburg?"

"West of here on the Chicago and Northwestern... 'bout an hour with all the stops."

"Do ya'll think Mason could've gone to find her?"

"Don't think so. He gave up on her when she left."

Clay wasn't ready to give up on this, though, quite so easily. He still believed that Toby was holding something back. "Can y'all think of anything else that might help us find him?"

"Look... I told ya before... I don't know any more. But you might wanna spend some time at the Red Brick Inn... a tavern over on Fourth Street."

"Why there?"

"The crowd that hangs out there usually knows all the gossip... what's going on around town."

"Alright, Toby... we'll go there. But if you hear anything, we're staying at the Cliff House at the lake."

They left Toby's house and headed back to downtown. Being a county seat, Baraboo was a fair-sized town, and its several blocks of two-story brick and limestone business district surrounding the courthouse square always seemed busy. During the day, buggies of all types and sizes lined the streets, and scores of people scurried about. Cops in khaki summer uniforms strolled the sidewalks with Colts hanging from their hips. But they were a pleasant lot, cordial, and the Montana lawmen that Clay and Christian knew would have them for breakfast.

Unlike Silver Spring, where the saloons and gambling joints howled nearly around the clock, Baraboo's taverns and saloons, including the Red Brick Inn on Fourth Street, were quiet this time of day. Nighttime, though, is when they came to life; the crusaders would just have to wait for a later hour when the place started to populate.

"You look lost," a voice said to them. Clay and Christian turned toward the man sidling up to them, his pork pie hat cocked at a comical angle, his weathered face nearly as wrinkled as his tan suit that smelled of stale beer and cigar smoke.

"Not lost, really... just looking for someone."

"Looking for someone," the man repeated. "Done my share o' that."

"What do y'all mean?" Clay wouldn't have chosen this creature out of a crowd to start a conversation, but during his time spent in saloons and gambling halls in the gold fields, he'd rubbed elbows with a lot worse.

"Fact is, when I was a youngun, I thought I wanted to be a preacher, but then the war come along and that all changed."

"War? Y'all mean between the States?"

"Certainly."

"Blue or gray?"

"Blue, o' course. Joined up with the Iron Brigade... Wisconsin's finest. Anyhow, when I come home after the war, I figured I'd had a part in too much killin' already, so instead of savin' souls I started trackin' the ones that couldn't be saved."

"Y'all mean... like criminals?"

"That's right... made my livin' as a bounty hunter."

"Did ya capture a lot of 'em?" Christian asked.

"My share. Had t' kill a few, too... the ones that weren't willin' to come in peaceable."

"Sounds like an interesting life."

"Was... but I give it up... started t' get too dangerous."

"I know what y'all mean by that."

"But just now, I thought you might be willin' to pay a silver dollar for a bit of information you need to know."

"What kind of information? And what makes y'all think I can just toss over a silver dollar to someone I don't know?"

"Oh... a southern gentleman like yourself paired up with this big city dandy? I seen ya play-actin' out at the Chateau by the lake... tellin' ever'body you was part of a theater troupe come here from Montana to entertain folks with vaudeville comedy and song. So, first off, I'd bet you could part with a silver dollar, and second, the information could save your life, but the only way you'll find out is to hand over the silver first."

"Y'all trying to fleece me?"

"No, sir. Not at all. John Helge is an honest man. I'm tryin' to be your friend. I gotta eat, too, ya know."

Clay dug in his pocket, pulled out the coin and held it up for John to see. "If this is some kind of trick, y'all will be sorry." He flipped the silver dollar in the air and John caught it as if he'd had a lot of prac-tice. "Now, what's the information y'all have that will save me and my friend from an untimely end?"

"You're bein' followed."

Christian's face turned somber. "We are?" he mumbled.

Clay remained steadfast with his usual poker face.

"Don't turn around to look... just casually glance to your left. At the store entrance across the inter-section you will notice a fellow of certain reputation in this town."

Clay glanced to his left, and then quickly looked back to John. "That's Jasper Blackburn."

"Yes, and he's been followin' you since you left the train depot this morning. You know him?"

"Sort of... we had a brief but disturbing encoun-ter a couple of weeks ago. How do y'all know he's fol-lowing us?"

"I was walkin' past the depot and I noticed him watchin' you in a peculiar fashion, and when he started followin' you at some distance, I followed him. Thought it was strange. Does he pose a threat to either of you?"

"Perhaps. What do y'all know about him?"

"Only that his father has had to bail him out of jail a few times, and has called in a favor now and then to keep the lad out of jail... too many fights and broken skulls, too many girls that didn't belong to him, and then there was the vandalism to the Catholic Church... I was raised Lutheran, mind you, but defacing *any* church doesn't sit good with me."

Clay and Christian suddenly realized that John Helge was, perhaps, more sincere with his friendship than they had first imagined. Jasper Blackburn *could* be a threat.

"I suspect," Clay said, "that Jasper Blackburn might be responsible for the odd disappearance of another friend of ours. Marty Mason was supposed to start as our piano man, but he has mysteriously vanished."

"I'll keep an ear to the gossip mill," John said. "I'll let you know if I turn somethin' up."

"I'm Clay Edwards, and this is Christian Parker. We're staying at—"

"The Cliff House," John finished. "I know."

EIGHTEEN

They watched John walk away and disappear into the next block to the west. He was truly an unusual person, but they were glad they had met him. As for Jasper Blackburn, they sensed his eyes still upon them; a brief glimpse toward Fourth and Oak found him, but now he had crossed the street, coming nearer. Clay winked at Christian and urged him to cross the street. "Let's see if Roscoe is interested in having something to eat with us... I'm hungry."

When they reached the opposite sidewalk another man fell in step with them. "I see you just met Mr. Helge... quite a character, isn't he?"

This man had a more distinguished look about him, brown felt bowler hat with a colorful pheasant feather tucked in the band, a strikingly squared jaw

line that gave the three-piece brown suit, white collar
and string tie an appearance of authority.

"Yes," Clay replied. "John is a very interesting
man."

"And do you have business here in Baraboo, Mr.
Edwards?"

Christian gave a startled stare.

Clay just smiled. "Y'all are the law."

"Yes, I am, but how could you tell?" The man
didn't seem at all surprised that Clay had branded
him a law officer, even though he didn't display any
identifying badge; he didn't even carry a weapon, although Clay was certain there must be a revolver inside his coat.

"Perhaps the same informant that gave y'all my
name."

"Ah, but Mr. Edwards, your reputation precedes
you—gambler, entertainer—and I guess it would be
fitting that a man of your nature would have a nose
for the law. Allow me to introduce myself." He offered his right hand as they continued around the
corner. "I'm Chief of Police Daniel Rowley."

"Pleased to meet y'all, Chief. This is my friend
and stage partner, Christian Parker."

They shook hands.

"We keep a respectable town here, gentlemen, so
while you're here—"

"Oh, Chief, sir," Clay interrupted. "Don't worry
about us. But we are concerned about a friend who
seems to have disappeared."

"Oh? Someone missing?"

"Yes. His name is Marty Mason."

Chief Rowley stopped abruptly at the walkway to the courthouse steps. He gave a little chuckle. "Marty Mason? Ellie Mason's kid?"

Clay had to think a moment. "Eleanor... yes."

"Marty Mason has disappeared so many times, they should've made him a magician at the circus instead of a piano player. He always shows up again in a day or so."

"I guess, then, that y'all wouldn't be concerned that no one has seen him since Monday."

"Like I said, gentlemen. Marty Mason always shows up. Now if you'll excuse me, I have some business to attend to in the courthouse." And then he was gone.

When the chief was out of earshot, Christian said "Well, it doesn't look like we'll get any help from the police."

"Didn't expect to. And now we have to handle Jasper Blackburn."

It was Clay's intention to walk right up to Jasper and confront him out in the open, in plain sight of at least twenty people on the street. But just then was when the shooting started. Several gunshots in rapid succession echoed between the buildings; Clay spotted the man coming out of the bank with a gun in his hand and a black kerchief over his face, apparently the source of the commotion.

"So much for a respectable town," said Christian. He turned quickly to see Jasper retreating in haste. Then more shots came as the gunman scattered lead randomly in all directions, an effective means to clear the streets. Women screamed as the men folk grabbed them and hurried them off to take cover.

Two more masked bandits exited the bank, one firing shots into the bank, and the other firing over the heads of the screaming crowd trying to flee. Glass windows shattered and bullets ricocheted off brick walls. It sounded like a major battle. Then a masked rider emerged from the alley leading three more saddled horses. He fired several shots into the street with a Winchester to clear the way as the gunmen on foot kept shooting, running to the waiting mounts.

Police Chief Daniel Rowley ran from the courthouse toting a Winchester rifle, bravely taking up a position on the sidewalk across from the bank. He aimed and fired a couple of shots, wounding one of the riders.

Clay started toward the melee, but Christian grabbed his arm to stop him. "Are you crazy? They have Winchesters in case you didn't notice."

Clay easily wrestled away from Christian. "I have to help the chief" was all he said, and then turned to see Rowley take a bullet in the arm, knocking his rifle to the ground and slamming him against a wall. The gunman charged his horse toward the chief, Winchester pointed, ready to finish the job when Clay, only ten yards away, leveled his .45 and squeezed off a single shot. The rider toppled off his horse and landed on the dusty ground, never to move again. Clay aimed where the other riders had been, but by then they had fled southward and were headed out of town.

Blue gun smoke and dust hung in the still air as near silence engulfed the town. Pure shock was the general feeling as people began slowly creeping back into the street, curious of what had just happened.

Clay hurried to Chief Rowley. "How bad is it?" he asked.

Rowley already had a handkerchief wrapped around his bleeding arm. "Not too bad… just a flesh wound. A lot less damage than what you laid on him." He nodded toward the motionless bandit lying in the dirt, and then stood up. He and Clay slowly walked over to the body. Rowley reached down and slipped the kerchief mask from the dead man's face. A curious, mumbling crowd gathered around.

"Frank Corelli," someone said, and several hands were patting the chief's shoulder and Clay's.

Rowley solemnly stared at Clay. "Thanks."

Within a short time the grave silence was replaced by near chaos; crying and screaming and shouting erupted as the reality of the situation set in. The bank had been robbed, and people were injured and dead; the comfort of safety in the town had been compromised. Store owners stood outside their establishments with loaded weapons ready to defend but too late to do any good, watching confused and dazed citizens wondering what they should do next.

Clay picked up the Winchester that lay just inches from the dead man's outstretched arm, stepped back to the sidewalk; Chief Rowley, his sleeve red with his own blood, picked up his rifle and headed briskly to the bank.

As the disorder continued among the people on the street, Christian found Clay, and they watched as four men hoisted the body into a wagon. Clay stepped forward and laid the Winchester beside the body. "This was his," he said, and then stepped back to Christian's side.

"I saw what you did." Christian said. "You saved the chief's life. He should be grateful."

Clay stood there silently for a while, reflecting on the past few minutes. It had all happened so fast. The visions of the whole ordeal replayed over and over in his head, and he didn't like what he saw.

He snapped out of the reverie, and then he spoke to Christian without looking at him: "Let's go to Connor's store."

They started walking down Oak Street, the bank on the opposite side where a large crowd was gathering. A pathway opened up for a doctor and two nurses to get inside, and then abruptly closed in again behind them. Obviously, there were injured victims in the bank needing medical attention; Clay pushed onward to the next block, Christian following. There was no point in joining the mob, only to add to the confusion.

Men, women, and children were still running—some away from the scene, some toward it, some to reach a parked buggy or wagon. Up ahead, Clay saw Roscoe standing at the mercantile entrance, anxiously looking toward the bank area, a shotgun clenched in his right hand, just like many other storekeepers they had already passed.

"I don't think you need that anymore," Clay told Roscoe as he and Christian stood beside him. "They're gone now."

"I heard one of the bank robbers was shot dead."

"It was Clay," Christian said.

Roscoe's eyes widened as he turned his head to look at Clay. "You shot one of the robbers?"

"He was going to kill the Police Chief... I had to."

Roscoe's frown was traded for an admiring smile, for he was truly gazing upon his hero. He glanced down to see the slight bulge in Clay's coat. "The Smith and Wesson?" He had seen the remarkable weapon once when Clay showed it to him at the Cliff House, and now he was even more impressed.

Clay nodded. "Uh-huh."

Christian Parker had gotten used to Clay's practice of late to carry the .45 revolver under his coat. It was much like when he'd first met Clay back in Silver Spring, Montana; there it was common for most everyone to carry a sidearm—concealed or not—but here, it was rare. But he saw Clay in a different way than most people did. To him, Clay was like one of those dime novel outlaws that you like and admire, because that fictional character has that good side that doesn't hurt anyone undeserving of harm, and is the first to help out a poor soul in need. Clay was a gambler —or, ex-gambler—with his share of dark history. However, that was behind him now, and Christian saw him in this new light. Judging by Roscoe's expression at that moment, he knew that Roscoe saw him that way, too, even though he was aware of Clay's past.

Mr. Connor came walking briskly down the side-walk.

"Pop!" Roscoe said. "I was worried. Were you at the bank?"

"Yes, I just came from there. Let's all go inside," Mr. Connor urged with a troubled look on his face.

The store was completely void of any customers, but that was no surprise considering the circum-stances. Everyone in town was more drawn to the situation at the bank than browsing among flour sift-ers and bed linens.

Roscoe replaced the shotgun to its discreet perch under the front counter just below the cash register. Mr. Connor stood behind him, mopping his brow with a white handkerchief.

"So, what happened at the bank?" Roscoe asked.

Mr. Connor put the handkerchief back in his coat pocket. "I didn't see what was happening at first... I had my back to it all, and then I heard a woman scream and one of the robbers pointed a gun at the teller, demanding access to the safe. I was so fright-ened that I didn't hear what all was said. There were two more robbers each waving two pistols at every-body in there. Then... I don't know... maybe three minutes later the first robber came out carrying a bag... I suppose filled with money... and the next thing I knew, the shooting started."

"The robbers? Or somebody else?"

"I don't know for sure... the robbers, I guess." Mr. Connor wiped his forehead with the handkerchief again. "It all happened so fast. I ducked down on the floor... just like the other people in there did... and there were more shots fired during the next few seconds... and then it got quiet in there... I guess the robbers went out and jumped on horses. I could hear a lot of shooting from outside, but I didn't get up to look. No one did."

"Did y'all recognize any of them?" Clay asked.

"The robbers? No... they all had masks."

"One of the robbers was shot and killed," Roscoe informed his father, but he decided not to reveal the marksman just then. The word would get out soon enough.

"Yes, I heard someone say that afterward."

"Was anybody in the bank hurt?"

Mr. Connor grimaced at the question from his son. "Yes... I'm afraid so. Three seriously wounded... and two dead... that I know of... Sam Johnson and another man I didn't recognize."

Roscoe put an arm across his father's shoulders. "Sam Johnson? That's awful... but, Pop, I'm glad you're safe."

"Thank you, Son. Now if you don't mind watching the store for a while longer by yourself, I'm going upstairs to lie down for a while." He nodded to Clay and Christian. "Please, excuse me, gentlemen. It's been a dreadful morning."

"We're glad y'all are okay," Clay said.

"Get some rest," Christian added.

They heard heavy footfalls on the steps to the Connors' upstairs dwelling; a door opened and closed. Roscoe could imagine Pop hugging his wife, and then telling her the bad news.

"Your Pop is a lucky man," Christian told Roscoe.

"Yeah... I could've lost him."

A dark shadow passed over Clay's expression; both Roscoe and Christian noticed; could it be that he, too, just didn't feel well after his experience? Obviously, something was troubling him.

"Are you okay?" Roscoe asked. "Would you like to rest in my room upstairs?"

"No, I'm fine." Clay dug out his pocket watch to check the time. "We should be getting to the depot."

NINETEEN

Thunderous dynamite booms at the nearby quartzite mine rattled the dishes on the breakfast table. No matter how many times he heard and felt the blasts, Christian always flinched at the sound. The others had become accustomed to the noise and vibrations, only raising a few eyebrows, so Christian's reactions were usually amusing to them. They didn't realize, this particular time, that the prior day's experience had put him on an extra sharp edge.

News of the bank robbery had already circulated at Devil's Lake Village. So when the entire cast of the Silver Spring Players gathered on Saturday morning for breakfast in the hotel dining room, it seemed the only thing they didn't know was that Clay had been the one who'd saved Chief Rowley's life.

"Do you suppose they have any suspects," Victor wondered.

"Well, they have one," Henry replied. "The one that got shot by some hero on the street."

"But he's dead," Clyde said. "And dead men don't talk."

"It was Clay!" Christian blurted out. He couldn't hold it back any longer. "Clay was the hero on the street. We were right there when it happened."

Everyone at the table turned their heads and stared first at Christian, and then at Clay.

"Is that true?" Charlotte asked.

"I'm afraid it is," Clay responded.

"You had your forty-five?" Henry said.

"Yeah…"

"When did you start carrying a gun again?" Victor asked.

"Since we've been looking for Marty Mason."

"Why?"

"Because the scoundrel who's probably responsible for Marty's vanishing act doesn't play fair. The *equalizer* evens the odds."

Henry threw Clay a curious stare. "You suspect that our new piano man is involved in some foul play?"

"If y'all mean to say 'Is Marty the *victim* of foul play?' my answer to that is yes."

"And do you think this *scoundrel* you speak of is mixed up in the bank robbery?"

"No… Christian and I saw him on the street at the very moment the bank was getting held up."

"And he turned tail and ran when the shooting started," Christian added.

"And you shot one of the bank robbers," Henry said.

"He'd already wounded the Police Chief in the arm... and he fully intended to murder him next... I had to."

"It's true," Christian confirmed. "I saw it all."

"So," Victor said. "Now I suppose the newspaper reporters will be swarming in here next."

"Never know..." Henry said. "Could be good publicity for our new theater..." He raised his water glass as if to make a toast with a theatrical flair. "To the actor who gunned down a threat to society."

The wheels in Victor's head were definitely turning at a high rate of speed. "You know? This is beginning to sound like a good stage play. I should start writing..."

"Has anyone seen Simon this morning?" Christian asked.

"He said he was staying the night at a hotel in town," Vivian said. Then Claudia added: "He was meeting the carpenters at the theater early this morning. I do hope he arranges for some private dressing rooms."

Chatter continued during the rest of the meal, but now the conversations were directed away from the bank robbery and toward the speculations of a successful new opera house. Not that they disliked living in the hotel at the lake, everyone—especially the ladies—seemed anxious to settle into more permanent quarters in town. Only Clay and Christian thought they might miss the lakeside atmosphere.

They all agreed that on such a lovely day, it would be a good time for them all to enjoy a cruise around the lake together on the little steamer *Capitola*, in celebration of the new theater.

"I'll arrange it with the captain," Henry offered, "so we all can board at the same time."

As they whiled away the time on the Cliff House veranda waiting for their turn to board the boat, Clay noticed a familiar face coming toward them. Police Chief Daniel Rowley could have been there for any number of reasons, but considering the recent events, Clay felt confident that the chief was looking for him. When Rowley spotted Clay and stepped closer, Clay stood up and offered his right hand. "Good morning, Chief," he said. "How's the arm?"

"Good morning, Mr. Edwards. The arm is a little sore today, but the Doc says there shouldn't be any complications."

"That's good. Glad to hear it." Clay directed the chief's attention to the others. "Chief Rowley... I'd like y'all to meet the rest of the Silver Spring Players." He introduced each one by name as they stood in a semi-circle and shook hands with Rowley.

"I'm pleased to meet all of you, and I'm glad that you're all here together."

"We're going for a cruise around the lake on the Capitola. Would you care to join us?"

"Oh... no... actually, I'm afraid my visit to you to-day isn't exactly pleasant; I'm sad to say that I am the bearer of some bad news."

All curious eyes were now on the chief.

In a sorrowful voice, Rowley went on. "I regret to tell you that Mr. Simon Bordeaux was one of the victims at the bank robbery yesterday. He is dead."

It only took a few seconds for the astonished expressions to appear, and then the sobs from Claudia and Vivian poured out; Charlotte fell back into her chair and covered her face with her hands. Clyde rushed to her, kneeled beside her and put his arms around her. Clay and Christian, Claudia and Vivian, all engaged in a comforting group embrace. Henry and Victor removed their hats and held them to their chests. No one spoke for several minutes.

Finally, Henry quietly said: "I'll go cancel our boat cruise," and he started his walk to the dock.

"Shall I walk you to your room?" Clyde asked Charlotte.

She only nodded her approval. He helped her up from the chair and they walked away.

"Let's go to our room, too," Vivian told her sister.

"We'll walk with you," Christian said, and he and Clay escorted the women toward the hotel entrance.

"Mr. Parker," Chief Rowley called out.

Christian stopped and turned.

"Please come back when you can... I'll wait. I need to talk to you."

Christian nodded, turned, and continued on with Claudia.

That left only Victor with Chief Rowley. "Do you have any suspects?" Victor asked.

"We do. They rode south out of town... one has a severe gunshot wound, and he probably won't make it too far. The county sheriff has a posse out. It's just a matter of time until they catch up with them."

Henry returned from the boat dock about the same time Christian and Clay came back from escorting Claudia and Vivian to their room.

"How 'bout a good stiff drink?" Henry said to Victor. "I have a bottle of Scotch in my room."

"Yes," Victor replied. "We can leave Christian to his business with Mr. Rowley."

The two of them wandered off.

"You said you wanted to see me," Christian said.

"Yes," Rowley replied. "If we could speak in private?"

"Anything you have to say to me, Chief, you can say in front of Clay."

"Alright, then. First of all, are you any kin to Mr. Bordeaux?"

"No... we've just been close... with the theater and all."

"Well, he must've considered you important."

"Why do you say that?"

"Because his last words to me were 'Give the key to Christian Parker.' Fortunately for me, because of our meeting yesterday, I knew who he meant. But the only key we found on his person—other than a hotel room key—was this." Rowley pulled from his coat pocket a gold key strung on a gold chain. "Do you recognize it?"

Christian stared at the key. "Yes. The chain was

around his neck, wasn't it?"

"Yes, it was." Rowley put both keys and chain in Christian's open palm. "I'm terribly sorry for your loss."

Christian closed his fingers around keys. He was fighting back tears.

Clay put a hand on Christian's shoulder. "Where can we find Simon's body... for burial?"

"The body is at the undertaker's parlor on Second Street."

"Thanks, Chief. We'll make the necessary arrangements."

"Alright, then. I will let the undertaker know. Now, I must bid you farewell, as I have other matters to attend to in town." He shook their hands and left.

"What do we do now, Clay?"

"Now that you have the key, we go open Simon's lock box, and then I guess we have to go see the undertaker and arrange a funeral."

TWENTY

They buried Simon Bordeaux's body the next afternoon. The undertaker hired a minister to perform a simple graveside service in a hillside cemetery overlooking Baraboo. The Players decided to keep it a small, private affair since they or Simon didn't know too many people here. Roscoe Connor and Chief Rowley attended, mostly out of respect.

When the ceremony was finished, the women in their black dresses and the men in their black suits didn't linger long, as it had already been a painful ordeal. The teary-eyed and silent mourners boarded the carriages awaiting the procession back to the depot.

But they hadn't been entirely alone in the hilltop graveyard. Clay wondered what interest Anton Helge would have in Simon's funeral, watching from afar, but because Chief Rowley was there, he kept his distance; there would be other opportunities.

"Well, that's that, then," Victor said while they waited for the next train. "Guess I'll be going back to Saint Louis."

"Yes," Henry said. "I'll be heading back to New Orleans. What are your plans, Clyde?"

"Charlotte and I have been discussing the possibilities of San Francisco."

Christian couldn't believe what he was hearing. "But what about our new theater?"

Victor put his hand on Christian's shoulder. "Christian, my boy... without Simon, there *is* no new theater."

"He's right," said Henry. "Simon was the businessman... he knew how to make things happen. None of us have those skills that he had, and I doubt that we could attain even a fraction of the success that Simon could have achieved."

"But we could try."

"If you want to try, Christian, we can't stop you, but you'll be on your own."

Later that afternoon, Clay and Christian lounged in their room at the Cliff House, not in the mood for any outdoor activities, even on such a warm May day. The others had all split up, each to their separate ways; Christian assumed they might be packing their belongings in preparation for travel to their next destinations. It was easy to understand that everyone's spirits were low; Simon had provided bright expectations, and there had been little doubt that another successful season was on the threshold. Now, all that had suddenly changed, and emotions could be nothing more than sorrow and disappointment.

Christian sensed something different in Clay,

however. Amidst the sorrow for Simon's death, there was something else that seemed just on the cusp of anger, difficult to define.

An unexpected knock sounded on the door. Thinking it must be one of the Players, Christian was astonished by the sight of the man he barely knew.

"Oh, I'm sorry. I thought this was Clay Edwards's room."

"It *is* Clay's room... and mine. What can we do for you, Mr.—I'm sorry... I don't remember your name."

"Helge... Anton Helge. I was hoping to have a chat with Clay."

Clay came to the door. "Anton. What a surprise. What brings y'all out here?"

"I heard 'bout your associate, Mr. Bordeaux... gettin' kilt at the bank."

"How did y'all know he was our associate?"

"Word gets 'round... y' know."

"I saw y'all watching us at the cemetery this afternoon."

"Yes... reckon you did... wanted to make sure the information was correct."

"What information?"

"That the deceased was a close associate of yours."

"Not only was he our associate... he was a dear friend... and the leader of our theatrical troupe."

"Yes, well, then maybe you'd be interested to see justice done. May I come in for a little more privacy?"

Clay gave Anton a curious stare and nodded.

"I mean... those robbers and murderers caught and brought in to get what they deserve," Anton said as he entered the room.

Christian watched and listened closely. With Clay's next words he began to see the anger coming out.

"I'd kill 'em myself if I got the chance. But I know that prob'ly won't happen. And besides... Rowley told us the county sheriff has a posse out huntin' 'em down."

"Only trouble is that posse's huntin' in the wrong direction."

"What d' y'all mean?"

"The posse is headed to Sauk... and maybe Lone Rock."

"Is that south?"

"Uh-huh."

"Well, that's the direction the robbers headed. I saw all three of 'em ride that way out of town... hell, everybody saw 'em."

"That's just what they wanted you and everybody else to see. Oldest trick in the book."

"So y'all are saying that they didn't go south."

"Nope. They surely didn't."

"So where'd they go?"

"Clay... I'm a bounty hunter. Bank's put up five thousand dollars reward money on them critters. I can't be spillin' out ever'thing I know quite so freely."

"But I thought y'all said ya gave it up."

"I did... but I thought I'd give it one last shot... providin' I had you for a partner. I heard 'bout you and the fourth robber."

Clay gave a look that could peel paint off a church. "What makes y'all think I wanna be a bounty hunter?"

"'Cause y' lost a good friend, and y' want justice. I can see it in your eyes, and I can hear it in your voice."

"Clay!" Christian said. "Don't—"

Then there was another knock at the door. Christian scowled at Clay; he clearly didn't approve of the risks Anton Helge was proposing. He stepped to the door and pulled it half open. "Toby!"

"I gotta talk to you," Toby said. "It's real important."

Christian swung the door open wider. "Come in."

Toby started to enter, but when he saw Anton, he stopped abruptly. "Oh... I didn't know someone else was here... I could come back—"

"Come in, Toby," Clay demanded. "I'm assuming y'all have some news about Marty?"

"Well... yeah... but if I'm interrupting something..."

"Not at all, Toby." Then Clay turned to Anton. "Excuse me, for a moment, but this is another pressing issue." Then he turned back to stare at Toby's cast. "How's the arm?"

"Okay... doesn't hurt so much anymore."

"That's good. Now, what d' y'all know about Marty Mason?"

"I heard about the bank robbery and your boss getting killed."

"Yeah..."

"And I heard about you shooting Frank Corelli after the hold-up."

"What does that have to do with Mason?"

"Frank Corelli worked for the Ringling Circus last season... on the canvas crew... him and Dobbs. They're from New York. Me 'n Mason chummed with 'em a lot during our off time."

Clay guided Toby to a chair. "Okay... so will y'all get to the point?"

"Frank 'n Dobbs came to see me about a week ago... had another pal from New York with 'em. They were real upset when they saw my arm in a cast, and when I told 'em that Mason wasn't around... that he'd joined up with your vaudeville act, they got real pissed off."

"So now we've identified at least one of the other bank robbers," Anton said.

"Why were they upset about Mason joining up with us?" Clay asked.

"Don't know," Toby replied. "But I'm afraid they might've done something bad to him."

Clay thought about the satchel he'd found in the bushes by the river; Toby's speculation was believable; and then the visions of the robbery replayed in his head again, and he saw the wild aggression in that desperado's eyes just before he squeezed the trigger of his forty-five. The sound of the blast jolted him back to the present.

He looked at Anton. "How far do we have to go?"

"An easy day's ride north."

"Clay," Christian pleaded. "Don't do this. Don't go chasing after bank robbers."

"This has gotten personal, Christian. They're not just bank robbers. They killed Simon. And they prob'ly kidnapped Marty. Don't y'all understand?"

"I understand that you'll be taking an incredible risk."

"It's a risk I'll have to take."

At that point, Christian realized there was no chance of convincing Clay to withdraw from Anton's proposal. His decision, right then and there, was final.

Yet another knock on the door.

"Who is it?" Clay called out.

"It's me... Roscoe," came from the other side.

Clay opened the door.

"I wanted to see how you're doing," Roscoe said.

"We're kinda busy right now, but come in. Did y'all arrive on the train?"

"No, on my horse." Roscoe, too, was surprised to see Anton Helge and Toby Atwood in the room. "Hello, Mr. Helge. Hi, Atwood." He looked at Clay as if to ask what they were doing there.

"Anton and I were just discussing some travel plans."

"Oh? Where are you going?"

"Anton seems to know where Simon's killers went, and we're going after them."

"Where?"

"A day's ride north, so says Mr. Helge. But he won't tell me any more."

Roscoe submerged himself in deep though. "Newport?" he said as he stared at Anton. "Of course... what a perfect hideout for thieves."

Judging by Anton's reaction, and his lack of response, Clay figured that Roscoe must be right. "Y'all know this place? What is Newport?"

"It's a ghost town... up on the Wisconsin River. I've gone fishing there a few times."

"Ghost town?"

"Yeah... it was a boomin' town at one time... the railroad promised to cross the river there, but it didn't... bypassed the town completely and built the bridge at Kilbourn. Now there's nothing left at Newport 'cept a few rickety old buildings and empty streets."

"We should leave at first light tomorrow," Anton suggested.

"No," Clay said. "We should leave now. They already have the advantage."

"There's not much daylight left."

"We'll camp along the way."

"I'm going, too," Roscoe announced.

Clay looked at Anton.

"Can y' use a gun?" Anton asked.

"Been shootin' rabbits since I was nine."

"Well... guess one more gun can't hurt. You two meet me at the livery stable in two hours. Bring a bedroll and some grub for breakfast... and wear a warm coat. It'll get chilly tonight."

TWENTY-ONE

When Anton and Toby had left, Christian, once again, tried to avert Clay and Roscoe from going on this manhunt for pestilent criminals. "It's a bad idea. Catching bank robbers and murderers is a matter for the police to handle," he declared. "These are some dangerous men you're going after... you could get killed."

But his pleading had as much affect as a stone tossed into a pond: it made a splash, and then disappeared.

Roscoe sat quietly, just listening and observing. He fully understood Christian's reservations, but he was determined to follow Clay's strong and bold perseverance, even if it was forbidding.

Clay continued to prepare for the trip, filling pockets with ammunition, rolling a couple of blankets, and finding his fleece-lined leather jacket. Then he turned to Roscoe. "Do y'all have a sidearm?"

"Just my hunting rifle... and this." He clumsily pulled a derringer from his coat sleeve.

Clay gave a little grin. "Christian... where do y'all keep your Colt thirty-eight?"

It was no use. Christian now knew there was no point in challenging Clay's objective; he would ride off to some unknown destination seeking Simon's killers, no matter what. "It's in the bottom of my trunk," he relented.

"Got any ammo for it?"

"There's a full box."

"Would y'all kindly get it and let Roscoe use it?"

Christian opened his personal belongings trunk and dug to the very bottom, bringing up the Frontier Colt .38, that Clay had convinced him to buy from a drifter needing cash. It was wrapped in an oil-stained white towel. He hadn't fired it since the day he acquired it—target shooting at bottles and tin cans propped up on a fence rail with Clay coaching him, and he hadn't carried it since he quit working at the Royal Hotel in Silver Spring.

He handed the pistol and box of cartridges to Roscoe. "Here... keep it... it's yours... it's in perfect working order... I don't want it anymore."

Roscoe stared at Christian questioningly, and then he glanced at Clay.

Clay shrugged his shoulders. "Go ahead. Take it. Doesn't do Christian much good buried in a trunk."

Roscoe took the gift in his hands, unfurled the

towel and inspected the weapon that still looked like new. He looked at Christian again. "But it's yours... I really can't—"

"Sure you can. You need it right now more than I do. I want you to have it."

"Thank you. I don't know what to say."

"You've said enough."

Clay looked at his pocket watch. "We should go. By the time we get to town and y'all get your gear, it'll be time to meet Anton. Where's your horse?"

"At a hitching post back of the hotel." Roscoe slipped the box of shells into a coat pocket and then stuffed the revolver under his belt. To offer assistance, Clay adjusted the gun's position a little, and then buttoned Roscoe's coat. "There," he said. "No one will ever know it's there."

Clay gathered up the bedroll and his leather jacket, and as he followed Roscoe out the door, Christian caught him by the arm, spun him around and hugged him. "Be careful," he whispered.

On the way into town, riding double on the spirited chestnut stallion, Roscoe and Clay formulated a story to tell Mr. Connor as to the reason Roscoe wouldn't be at the store next morning. Roscoe felt a little uneasy about not telling the whole truth of his absence and the real nature of the trip, but Clay convinced him that their story wasn't entirely a lie. "I'll handle it if y'all get nervous."

The sun was low in the western sky, painting a bank of cottony clouds in glorious shades of crimson and gold; the temperature had risen considerably that day, and now it seemed more like a day for a picnic. But there wasn't time for picnics now.

On a Sunday evening, there were very few people out and about on the streets of Baraboo. Clay hoped Anton Helge wouldn't keep them waiting. As he followed Roscoe up the stairs to the Connors' apartment, he thought about the disappointment Christian must be feeling, the other Players, all with plans to travel to other parts of the country. He thought about Marty's fate, and what he would have to say to him if he ever saw him again. And he wondered about his own future, now that the Silver Spring Players were breaking up for the second, and more than likely, the last time.

Roscoe swung open the door; Mr. Connor sat at a dining table reading a folded-up newspaper. "Hi, Son... Clay," he greeted. On the table was a spread of roast beef, boiled potatoes, corn and place settings for three. Mrs. Connor came from the kitchen with a plateful of sliced bread. "Oh..." she said. "You brought a friend. I'll set another place at the table."

They weren't counting on this; they had overlooked that it was suppertime. Roscoe looked at Clay. Clay looked at his watch. It was a five minute ride to the livery stable; they had a half-hour. Clay nodded, and then said: "But we'll have to eat quickly... daylight's wasting."

They all sat down to the wonderful meal. As Mr. Connor passed the bowl of potatoes to Clay he asked: "Why are you in such a hurry?"

"I'm not going to be at the store tomorrow, Pop. I'm riding with Clay to Kilbourn. We have to leave tonight."

"Kilbourn! For heaven's sake... why are you going to Kilbourn?"

"Clay has some important business there, and he doesn't know the way."

"Oh? What kind of business?"

"Jacob!" Mrs. Connor scolded. "His business is none of your business."

"That's okay," Clay answered. "It's some personal matters concerning Simon."

"Simon?"

"Mr. Bordeaux... the man who was killed at the bank. He was a close personal friend."

"Oh, yes... he was the proprietor of your vaudeville troupe, wasn't he?"

"Yes, sir."

"Well, then... I certainly hope Roscoe can be of service. He's been that way many times. When shall I expect your return?"

"No more than a couple of days, three at the longest, sir. Thank you."

"And Mom?" Roscoe said. "We'll be camping along the way, so could you put some food in a bag for us to take?"

When they had finished eating, Roscoe dashed into his bedroom, rolled up the heavy quilt from his bed and tied it with a couple of leather boot laces. He emerged toting the bedroll, his winter coat, and the hunting rifle.

"Why the gun?" Mr. Connor asked.

"Injuns and snakes. Y' never know."

Mrs. Connor came from the kitchen with a cloth bag. "There's some ham and bread and molasses cookies in here," she informed them. And here's a canteen of cold water."

Because Roscoe's hands were full, Clay took the flour sack with the food and the canteen. "Thank y'all, Ma'am," he said. "And thank y'all for the fine supper, too."

She smiled warmly. "You are quite welcome... anytime. And have a safe journey."

TWENTY-TWO

A nton Helge waited outside the livery stable with a third horse, saddled and ready to ride. "You fellas done dawdling?"

"Sorry if we're late," Roscoe said. "Mom insisted that we eat supper before we left."

"Was it worth it?"

"Absolutely," Clay testified.

"Got ever'thing y' need?"

"Warm coats, bedrolls, food."

"I see y' got one rifle... what is that?"

"Winchester Ninety-four Centennial, thirty-thirty," Roscoe replied.

"She's a beauty." Then Anton pointed to the horse he had ready for Clay. "There's a 'Seventy-three Winchester in the saddle holster for you, Clay. Oh... and by the way... you *do* know how to ride, don't you?"

J.L. FREDRICK

"I'm from the south, I lived in Montana... what d' y'all think?"

"Just checking."

When all the gear was secured, they mounted the animals and rode to the north. They passed by the cemetery where Simon was buried just a matter of a few hours ago. The sight of the fresh grave made Clay even more determined.

Anton led the way as the three riders entered into the forested rolling hills; he seemed to know exactly where he was headed. The trails weren't difficult to see even in the half-light of dusk. Now and then, they came to wide clearings and open prairieland where farmers had tilled the ground, and then they plunged into deep forest again.

"What did y'all mean when you said 'Injuns' back at your father's house?" Clay asked Roscoe.

Roscoe chuckled. "The Injun wars ended long ago," he explained. "But now and again you might run into a few... they're mostly friendly, though... the Ojibwa and the Chippewa that are still around. I just needed an excuse for the Winchester."

"Oh," Clay said. He was still suspicious, but he hoped *Injuns* weren't likely to complicate matters. He went back to his thoughts about Christian, the Players, and his own future again. Certainly, he would be moving in some other direction now—that is, if he didn't get ambushed and killed by the desperados he was after. But Anton knew what he was doing. After all, he was an experienced bounty hunter, and his skills had kept him alive so far.

Nightfall was nearly complete; it was getting too dark to continue on. Anton brought them to a standstill at the edge of a small stream. "We'll camp here for the night."

"How much farther is it," Clay asked.

"We're about half-way, I'd guess."

"Maybe a little more," Roscoe commented.

They took the saddles and the gear off the horses and tied them with ropes long enough for the animals to reach the water and plenty of long, dry prairie grass. The night air now chilled without the warming sunlight. Night sounds began to fill the darkness. Owls hooted, coyotes yapped and howled, and a soft breeze whispered through the treetops. Clay and Roscoe gathered a few fallen tree branches while Anton kindled a small fire with twigs and dry leaves. In a little while, the campfire had produced a good, hot bed of glowing embers, and to the three sitting around it, the warmth felt really good.

Out of the night came another sound—one they hadn't expected. Horse's hooves against the trail came nearer; Anton and Clay drew pistols, ready for the worst.

"Clay! Connor! It's me, Toby Atwood. Don't shoot!"

Toby dismounted and stood back from the fire, but close enough for the light to fully show him.

Anton and Clay holstered their weapons.

"Toby! What are y'all doin' here?"

"I followed you."

"Why?"

163

"I want to help."

"Toby... you have a busted arm."

"My arm is broken, but I'm not helpless."

Anton looked Toby up and down. "You're the feller that was at the hotel this afternoon."

"Yeah."

"You shouldn't be here. You should go back home."

Clay got to his feet and stood beside Toby. "It's dark and cold out here, Anton. He can stay the night." He turned to Toby. "Do y'all have blankets?"

"Yeah."

"Okay. I'll take care of your horse. Y'all get warmed up by the fire."

"But in the morning," Anton growled, "You head for home."

"But I have a gun, and I can shoot. Why can't I go with you?"

"'Cause it's too dangerous for a feller with a busted arm."

Clay got the blanket from the horse and draped it over Toby's shoulders. Then he led the horse to where the others were tied.

Toby kneeled by the fire with the blanket wrapped tightly around him. A few minutes later, Clay returned and settled in beside Toby again.

Anton wrapped himself in his blanket, leaned back against his saddle, and within a short time, the others heard him snoring.

"Toby," Clay spoke in a low voice, not to disturb Anton. "Why in heaven's name did y'all follow us out here?"

"Truth is," Toby said, "I thought I might get part of the reward money they're offering for bringin' in the bank robbers. Ma is apt to lose our house now that I'm outa work for all summer. Don't know what we'll do."

"Toby... I'm sorry... I didn't know."

"How could you?"

"I'll give y'all my share when this is all over."

Toby's eyes widened. "I don't expect you to do that."

Clay put his hand on Toby's shoulder. "I'm not doing this for the money. I'll do that for y'all... but y'all have to promise me that you'll go back home in the morning."

"But I wanna help."

"Toby... y'all could get hurt even worse, and then what good would y'all be to your mother?"

The reality of the situation overwhelmed Toby. He just shook his head; he had no more to say.

"Now, y'all lay down and try to get some sleep."

Once Toby was settled down, Clay moved closer to Roscoe.

"What are you gonna do now?" Roscoe asked. "I mean, now that Simon is... gone... are the rest of you gonna keep on?"

"I doubt it. Christian thinks we should, but all the others are sayin' they're leaving... Saint Louis, New Orleans, San Francisco..."

"What about you?"

"Don't know yet... s'pose I'll have to go somewhere."

"Wherever you go..." Roscoe hesitated a long moment. "Wherever you go, can I go with you?"

"But... Connor. What about the mercantile and your father? Y'all have a future there."

"I hate that place. I don't wanna be there. I can't stand being cooped up all day, every day in that store."

"Connor... do y'all really know what I am?"

"I think so..."

"I'm not a natural-born stage actor. It worked out for a while when the gamblin' got a little too dangerous and Christian rescued me from a bad ending. But poker's what I do best. I don't know where I'm headed next, but I know I want to see the world... London, Paris, Madrid... maybe even Hong Kong. I don't plan to settle down anywhere... anytime soon."

"But you see... that's the life I want, too. I want to see the world. I have money saved up, so I can pay my own way, and I would gladly be your servant... your slave... anything to get away from here."

Clay pitched some more wood on the fire. "Y'all are serious, ain't ya?"

"Please... let me go with you."

"I'll sleep on it... and speaking of sleep..."

They settled into their blankets and quilts.

"G'night Connor."

"G'night Edwards."

TWENTY-THREE

C hristian was at the depot to catch the early train into Baraboo. He hadn't slept well; the thought of Clay and Roscoe seeking a confrontation with hardened criminals had kept him in a sleepless, tossing and turning mode most of the night, and he'd been wide awake since before the birds started chirping their morning sere- nades. But there were things he had to do that day before the other Players left; if he could, somehow, take over the contract for the building that Simon had purchased, perhaps there was a chance that he could convince the others to stay.

The train was right on time; as usual, a lot of cheerful people got off, eager to begin their stay at Devil's Lake Village and many were boarding, starting their journeys home. While he stood in line to board the coach, Christian thought about Clay; he wondered—he hoped—that Clay was being cautious, and that he would return safely, with or without the success of the mission. Somehow, though, he sensed that he and Clay were drifting apart; Simon's death had changed Clay, as if his interest in the theater had diminished. If the other Players left, there would be little hope of keeping Clay there, either.

During the short ride to the Baraboo station, for those few minutes, Christian tried to enjoy the passing scenery as the train chugged its way through the hills. The forest was getting greener, and patches of white and blue and yellow wild flowers dotted the hillsides. Spring was in full bloom.

He stepped off the coach at the Baraboo depot among a dozen or more passengers. By the time he walked to downtown, it was just about time for the bank to open. Several other men were gathered around the entrance, dressed in various attires from farm work clothes to business suits, apparently waiting for the bank to open. The conversations among them were about the robbery that had taken place there; they wondered how it would affect the financial well-being of the community; they wondered if the sheriff had been successful yet in capturing the thieves; Christian even heard the name *Bordeaux* mentioned.

And then came the snap of the lock as someone from inside turned the key to unlock the door. The bank was open for business.

He waited his turn to talk with a teller. "Hello... my name is Christian Parker."

"How do you do, Mr. Parker. What can I do for you?"

"I would like to talk to somebody about the building that Simon Bordeaux purchased. He was here to sign some papers on Friday... and he was killed during the hold-up."

"Oh, yes... Mr. Bordeaux... most unfortunate... you should probably talk with Mr. Norman Landry. He handles all of the real estate business."

"Where can I find Mr. Landry?"

The teller pointed. "His office is right over there."

"Thank you."

Christian walked across the large room to a row of small offices along the far wall. Norman Landry's name was on one of the doors. He knocked.

"Come in," a voice said. It sounded pleasant enough.

"Hello, Mr. Landry. My name is Christian Parker."

Norman Landry offered his hand across his big shiny desk. "Hello, Mr. Parker. How can I be of assistance?"

"I'm here about the building that Simon Bordeaux purchased to be used as an opera house."

Upon hearing the name Bordeaux, Landry's face turned solemn. "And why might you be interested in that?"

"Well, you see, Mr. Bordeaux was the leader of our theatrical troupe..."

"I see. And you are a part of that troupe?"

169

"Yes, sir... actor and singer. Clay Edwards and I came here from Montana last fall with Simon, and the other performers came this spring."

"Yes... that's just exactly what Mr. Bordeaux told me."

"So now, all the other performers are talking about going other places, now that Simon is gone. But if I can assume the responsibility of the theater operation, maybe I can convince them to stay."

Mr. Landry leaned back in his chair. "Well, Mr. Parker, there's just one little problem."

Christian's heart sank. He had hoped that Simon's deal could still be executed, that he could assume the contract, and with a little effort on his part, he could learn how to run a theater. But now there was *one little problem.*

Landry continued. "Mr. Bordeaux never signed the papers. The robbery interrupted all business that day—as you can well imagine—and he died before the deal was completed."

"So... he doesn't own the building?"

"No. I'm afraid not."

"Well... can I buy it?"

"I'm afraid you're too late, Mr. Parker. Another interested party that had the next option signed the papers Friday afternoon. The building is no longer for sale."

TWENTY-FOUR

Anton had thought to bring coffee. He cooked it in a little pot that he dug out of a saddle bag along with a couple of tin cups. Clay and Roscoe shared a cup. Toby didn't want any. It wasn't the greatest coffee—strong and bitter—but it was coffee.

"Oh, I meant t' tell ya last night," Toby blurted out as they all sat around the campfire. "I heard in town that the sheriff's posse found the bank robber that Chief Rowley shot... out at Parfrey's Glen... dead as a barn pole."

"Well," Anton said. "Now we know it's only two left."

"Yeah... they're sure it's two guys from New York."

"Now that you brought us that news, you're gonna git on that horse o' yours and ride back to Baraboo."

"But Mr. Helge... are y' sure I can't—"

"I'm dead sure... I don't want your blood on my hands."

Toby lowered his head, disappointment oozing out.

"C'mon, Toby," Roscoe said. "I'll help you with your saddle."

They got up from the fireside and went to the horses.

"So we got about four hours to go?" Clay asked.

"A little less... more like two."

"Y'all got a plan for when we get there?"

"Never make a plan 'til I see the situation."

"Think we can take 'em alive?"

"Don't know that 'til we get there."

"Y'all ever been to this ghost town before?"

"'Fore it became a ghost town... when I was a kid."

"So y'all know the layout."

"All different now. Most of what I remember is all gone."

Roscoe and Toby came back with Toby's horse saddled.

"Y'all ready to head back?"

"Guess so..."

"Remember what I told y'all last night."

"Yeah... thanks."

"Okay. We'll see y'all back in Baraboo."

"Yeah... see ya." Toby mounted his horse and rode away.

The last mile crossing over the moraines was the toughest part of the ride. Anton had chosen to leave the regular trail for their final approach. "If they're in there," he said, "They could be watchin' the trail."

At the crest of the last hill, a glimpse of the Wisconsin River could be seen through the trees, its sheer yellow sandstone banks rising fifty feet above the water on the other side. Below the hill was a mill pond, but nothing remained of the mill but a few foundation rocks. Beyond that lay a dusty strip that Anton pointed out as Main Street, and the few relic structures that had once been part of the business district of Newport.

"There's no way to get in there without being seen," Roscoe said. "Once you get across the bridge over Dell Creek, there's no place for cover 'cept those trees down by the river."

"Looks deserted. Y'all sure they're in there?"

"They're there, alright," Anton assured. "See the horse tracks from the buildings to the creek? They're takin' the horses down there for water."

"Maybe we should wait for that."

"Prob'ly doin' it in the dead o' night. We'd never see 'em."

It was time to summon up every ounce of courage they had. Anton knew what they would have to do. "Best way to find out where they are... is for me to just walk down there like I own the place. If they see me and start shootin' you two can follow the gunfire 'n sneak 'round behind the building they're in. They'll be watchin' me and won't know you're there."

"And what if you get hit?" Roscoe asked.

"That'll be my problem to deal with. You just get in behind 'em and take 'em by surprise."

"Y' mean... shoot 'em?"

"Yeah, Connor... think y'all can do that?"

"I... I... I guess so."

"Mr. Connor," Anton said. "Just remember... these guys are killers. They've killed before, and they'll kill again. If you don't shoot them, they'll shoot you. Now, which would you prefer?"

"They killed Simon," Clay added. "Remember?"

"Yeah, I remember."

"Okay... I'm gonna cross the bridge and head for the first building on the left. If there's no gunfire yet, it means they didn't spot me, 'n you two should be able to get across the bridge. I'll move up Main Street... try to draw some fire. You know what to do then."

Clay and Roscoe nodded. They all rode down the hillside to the edge of the tree line and dismounted. Anton tied the reins to a sapling and pulled his rifle from its scabbard. He took a deep breath. "You boys ready?"

They nodded, and Anton started walking. He was nearly to the bridge when Clay heard some leaves rustle behind him. He quickly turned to look. "Toby! What are y'all doing here?"

"I couldn't just leave... knowing that you might need another gun."

There wasn't time to argue. "Well, y'all are here now, so here's the plan." Clay explained the strategy, all the while keeping an eye on Anton's progress. "Y'all said y' have a gun?"

Toby pulled from a pocket a Baby Dragoon, a Colt

designed for use by the cavalry during the Civil War, a small gun effective at close range but not much more. "It was my grandpa's."

Anton reached the first building on the left. There had been no shots fired. He waved and pointed to the building across Main Street. Then he saw Clay and Roscoe hustling from the tree line toward the bridge, followed by a third... with a cast on his right arm. Anton shook his head in disgust. "What the hell..."

When his backup men had reached their destination across the street, Anton stepped out from behind the wall and cautiously moved forward. Clay peeked around the corner to watch for any other activity. When the two shots sounded, he spotted a bluish puff of smoke at a dark window three buildings up. By the sound, the shots were from two guns, each with a different report. One bullet kicked up dirt and dust at least twenty feet short and to the right of Anton; the other struck directly behind him, apparently just missing its target. A third shot, however, did find its target, striking Anton in his left leg just above the knee.

Clay spoke softly to Roscoe. "They're in the third building on the left. Anton is hit." Roscoe instantly ran to the back of the building and turned the corner. Clay knew he was headed in the right direction. Before he could tell Toby to stay put, and then make a dash across the street to help Anton to cover, Toby was already on a dead run to Anton. Amidst bullets kicking up bursts of dust all around him, he helped

Anton to his feet, and with his good arm around the wounded man, together they hobbled to the nearest alley between two buildings.

When Clay saw they were safely behind the wall, out of the line of fire, he turned and ran to the back of the building, heading the same direction that Roscoe had gone. As he ran, he heard more shots, this time from three different weapons; one of them had to be Roscoe's Winchester.

He stopped at the corner of the third building he passed, peering down the narrow alleyway. Roscoe wasn't there. The sun was hot and sweat trickled down his forehead into his eyes; he felt his heart pounding. Then three more shots echoed—a smaller caliber gun, perhaps the .38 or Toby's Baby Dragoon. It was nearly impossible to tell where the shots were coming from. The robbers had definitely been surprised by the intrusion, but the surprise was over; now they were using their cover, hidden inside one of the buildings to full advantage.

Clay knew he had to get across the street and to the rear of the building where the robbers were holed up; his best chance was to circle around far enough down the street where he wouldn't be noticed. But there were only two more buildings on his side, three on the other. And where was Connor? The silence for the next few minutes was almost eerie.

Clay darted across the alley to the rear of the next building, stopped and listened. He heard running footfalls and more rapid gunfire. Looking around the corner, he caught a glimpse of Connor sprinting to the other side of the street, and then he disappeared between two buildings there.

A minute later, Clay heard more shots, but they were somewhat muffled, as if they were coming from behind the building across the street. Connor had drawn the robbers away from the Main Street windows. Now was Clay's opportunity to get over there. With .45 extended, ready to fire at any moment, he dashed across, positioning himself flat against the front wall next to the doorway. He held his breath and listened. For the moment, there was no shooting, but he heard hastened footsteps on the wood floor inside. Sounding as if they were coming toward him, Clay pulled back the hammer of his .45. But then the footsteps seemed get more distant, and then came the crashing sound of another door opening. Clay quickly maneuvered to the window, the shattered glass panes strewn on the ground at his feet. Just as he looked inside he saw the back side of the dark gray coat and trousers scurrying out the side door. It was the same gray suit he'd seen on the rider bringing the horses out from the alley during the bank hold-up—not Simon's killer.

But the one left inside the building probably was, and right now he posed a deadly threat to Connor. Clay stepped back in front of the door and gave it a hard kick. As the door swung open he took three quick strides to get inside. In one instant he saw through the open side door another open doorway of the next building. In the next instant, he saw the man at the back window with the rifle. Startled by the front door crashing open, the man swung his rifle around and fired. Clay heard the bullet zing past his left ear. But before the man could lever another cartridge into the chamber of his Winchester, Clay squeezed off two shots. The force of the slugs knocked the man against the wall; a moment later, he was sprawled on the floor.

Clay walked cautiously to him. He kicked the Winchester away, and then he kicked the man in the ribs, checking for any reaction. There was none. Then he went to the open window. "Connor," he said in a barely audible tone. "Y'all okay?"

Roscoe recognized Clay's voice, and it seemed safe to raise his head up to the window to peer in. He gazed about the poorly-lit room. "Where's the other one?"

"Gone for now," Clay replied. He stepped closer to the window. "Anton and Toby are between the second and third buildings. Anton took a bullet in the leg. Go tell Toby to get his horse and ride as fast as he is able back to Baraboo and get Chief Rowley out here."

"What about the other one?"

"Don't worry 'bout him... just go tell Toby."

Reluctantly, Roscoe turned to go, and then he turned back to Clay. "Are you okay?" he said.

"Yeah, Connor... I'm fine."

Then Roscoe was gone.

TWENTY-FIVE

With his .45 still at the ready, Clay went to the open side door, looked both ways down the empty alleyway, and then studied the doorway across from him. Unlike the building he was in—all one big open room—the next one appeared to have been a saloon with a bar and a back room. He crossed the alley; trying not to make any noise, he stepped onto the threshold, glancing to the right and left. Large front windows facing Main Street let in a fair amount of light. To the left was a doorway into another room; to the right a staircase with a landing midway led to a second floor balcony. Straight ahead, a bar ran about half the length of the room. *Lots of places for him to hide,* Clay thought.

This is where they had set up camp for the time they had been there; on a table sat a box with a couple of cans of beans, a few slabs of beef jerky, some stale bread. A hunting knife was stabbed into the table top. Scattered on the floor were several empty bean cans and what appeared to be chicken bones. Two half-full bottles of liquor stood on the bar.

Clay thought first to check behind the bar. Someone could easily be crouched down out of sight back there. He was still quite certain there was only one more to find. Slowly he sidestepped around the table and chairs, frequently glancing to the upstairs balcony. As he inched his way to the end of the bar, he thought he heard a noise like a shoe scraping on a floor, a noise that he was sure he hadn't made himself. But he couldn't be sure where it had come from.

Nervous sweat rolled down his forehead and cheeks, and his shirt was soaked; he silently admitted to himself that this was, perhaps, the most precarious situation he had ever experienced, and he suspected the person he had cornered in this building shared similar feelings. Never in his wildest imagination did Clay ever expect to be in this position, but there he was, very near a showdown, and he hated the thought of what the outcome might be. He felt confident of his ability in this predicament; if his theory was correct, beyond doubt, he held the advantage—his opponent was not an expert gunman. But one fact couldn't be overlooked: even a novice can get off a lucky shot. He had to remain focused. The slightest distraction could mean life or death... for one of them.

He was just inches away from discovering what— if anything—was waiting for him behind the bar. An element of surprise would work to his advantage. With the Smith & Wesson cocked and pointed he took a deep breath and then one quick step to his right. He stood rigidly for a long moment staring at nothing but a bare, dusty floor.

A rush of air passed his lips as he released his held breath; his muscles relaxed just a little, but the tension remained. His eyes now focused on the doorway fifteen feet away at the other end of the bar leading into the back room. Then there was the sound of a squeaking floorboard, and Clay was certain that it had not come from overhead. The fourth member of the gang was in that back room, and by now, he had to be aware of Clay's presence.

Clay stepped gingerly toward the closed door, his pistol still poised. Stopping about six feet short of the wall, he listened again. Nothing. "I knew it was y'all," he said in a clam voice. "I don't want any more blood."

There was no response.

"If y'all have a gun... and I'm sure y' do... put it down and come out here where I can see you."

Still no response.

"Let's talk this out. No more shooting."

After a long wait, Clay heard a soft clunk that sounded like steel on wood. Then the door knob turned slowly and the door fell ajar. A Colt Peacemaker came sliding across the floorboards through the opening wide enough to let a dog through. "How did you know?" said a scared voice from beyond the door.

"I just did." Clay replied. He lowered the .45 to his side and sighed a breath of relief. "I recognized your cap."

The charcoal gray coat and trousers stepped timidly from out of the shadows and through the open door. It was the same suit Marty had put on the day he left to become the piano man for the Silver Spring Players. "I didn't want to do it," he said. His eyes were bloodshot and he looked like he hadn't slept for days.

"Why, then?"

"They kidnapped me on the way to the depot. Said they'd kill me *and* my mother if I didn't cooperate with 'em."

"But y'all knew them from the circus."

Marty nodded. "How'd you know that?"

"Toby Atwood. I was there on the street that day, Marty. I saw y'all bring the horses from the alley. And it was me who shot Frank."

Marty closed his eyes and lowered his head in shame. "I s'pose he talked."

"Frank was dead before he hit the ground."

Marty looked up again. "He's dead?"

"Yeah... and so's your other buddy... next door."

"Dobbs... I figured that much... when the shooting stopped. And he ain't my buddy."

"And the sheriff's posse found the other one south of town."

"Carmichael? Is he dead too?"

"Yeah... he was dead. But the worst part is... so is Simon Bordeaux."

Marty's eyes widened. "What... how?"

"Simon was in the bank to sign papers on our new theater. He got shot. We buried him yesterday."

Tears came to Marty's eyes. "I... I... didn't

know..."

"Marty... only because I know y'all didn't have anything to do with the killing... and I believe y'all were forced into this mess, I'm willing to turn my back if y'all want to walk out of here."

"But they'll hunt me down sooner or later."

"No they won't. Police and Sheriff are convinced it was three guys from New York they were after."

"The others... they *were* from New York."

"And they're certain that the fourth man is from New York, too."

"Fourth man... meaning me."

"Yes. And everybody... including your best friends and your mother and the police figure y'all are off on one of your sprees... not concerned... that y'all are gonna just turn up again one day like y'all usually do."

"How do you know that?"

"'Cause we've been looking for y'all, Marty. Remember? Y'all were supposed to be our piano man. Or has your new occupation blurred your memory? Christian and I spent days looking and talking to a lot of people. And in case you don't know... Connor and Toby were along on this hunt today."

"Connor and Atwood are here?"

"Yeah, but they don't know it's y'all we're looking for. Toby went back to fetch Chief Rowley"

"But Connor is here?"

"He's tending to Anton Helge just down the street a ways."

"Anton?"

"Yeah... your buddy Dobbs shot him."

"I need to talk to Connor."

"No, Marty... y'all can't do that."

"Why not?"

"He doesn't know y'all are mixed up in this. Y'all should clear out o' here before he does know."

"But where would I go?"

"Y'all got any money?"

"Yeah..."

"Bank robbery money?"

"No... my own... the bank money is hid under the bar." He pointed. "It's all there."

"Then get on your horse and ride to Kilbourn. They say it's not far from here. Get yourself a hotel room and lay low for a couple nights, buy some new clothes and burn that suit and cap y'all are wearing. And get rid of that horse, too. Then come back to Baraboo in a couple of days after this blows over, and y'all will be just fine."

"I don't know if I can do it."

"Sure y' can. It's that or be here when Chief Rowley arrives in a few hours... and he saw that gray suit, too."

"Clay? Does this mean we're still friends?"

"No, Marty... not like we were before."

"Then, why are you helping me?"

"'Cause I think it's the right thing to do. Now, get on your horse and ride."

TWENTY-SIX

When he was sure that Marty was well on his way, Clay went behind the bar to search for the bank loot. When he found it, he tossed the canvas bag on the table with the box of stale food. He looked around to make sure there was nothing left behind that could identify Marty. It would probably be the next day when Chief Rowley arrived from Baraboo; that would give Marty plenty of time to make himself scarce.

Clay felt justified in what he had done. Even though two innocent bystanders had died during the bank robbery that Marty had taken part in, he'd had no part in what happened inside. A jury, however, would probably not see it in that same light and Marty would suffer the consequences of the others' actions. Marty didn't deserve that. And now that all the money from the robbery was recovered, there was less chance that a full-scale manhunt would continue. Anyway, they were seeking a hardened criminal from New York, not a freckle-faced kid from their own town.

Now he had to contend with Roscoe Connor and

Anton Helge. But he had already figured out what to tell them. He stepped out into the sunlight; the fresh, cool breeze felt good.

"Did y' git 'em?" was Anton's first words when he saw Clay.

"One got away."

"Sure he's not hidin' somewhere right here?"

"Yeah... one horse is missing... he's long gone."

"We should go after him. Could y' tell which way he went?"

"Too many tracks in all directions... but we don't have to."

"Why not?"

"'Cause I found the bag of bank money."

Roscoe's eyes widened. "You found it?"

"Yeah... the bag's pretty plump... doubt if there's much missing."

Anton tried to stand up. His face twisted in a grimace from the pain in his leg. "We gotta try t' pick up his trail." But the wounded leg collapsed under him as soon as he tried to take a step. He let out a mournful groan as he tumbled to the ground.

"The only place y'all are going, Anton, is to a doctor."

"Toby and the chief won't be back for a long time," Roscoe said. "If we can get Anton on his horse... we could start back to Baraboo. Let's go get the horses."

Clay recognized Roscoe's eagerness, and his sudden willingness to abort the manhunt. "I s'pose we could."

They helped Anton to get comfortable again leaning against the wall. "Will y'all be okay if we go to bring the horses down here?"

"Yeah, yeah, yeah... but if I can ride to Baraboo, I could ride after that bank robber."

"Anton... that leg needs tending to..."

" Yeah, yeah, yeah... go get th' horses."

Roscoe was on his feet immediately, urging Clay along. They walked in silence to the bridge, and there Roscoe stopped.

"That was a pretty nice thing you did."

"What do y'all mean?"

"For Marty."

Clay's poker face remained. "Don't know what y'all are talking about."

"I heard you talking to him."

Clay stared at the ground, scraped the dirt with his boot.

"I came back to help you... that's when I heard you and Marty talking."

Clay gazed off into the distance.

"Were you gonna tell me?"

"No... I wasn't."

"Why not?"

"'Cause he's your best friend."

"How long have you known that Marty was involved?"

"Since the day of the robbery... I knew it was him on that horse coming out of the alley."

"Why didn't you say something?"

"'Cause I didn't really want to believe it myself... and if I had been wrong..."

"So are we gonna go on keeping it a secret?"

"Marty was forced into helping them... to keep his mother safe... didn't have anything to do with Simon getting killed, and I don't think he deserves to go to jail over it."

"So what are we gonna do?"

"Don't know 'bout y'all, but I'll be leaving here soon. I guess it'll be up to Marty."

They started for the horses again.

"What about Christian and the others?"

"The others are already planning to go back to where they came from. Christian? Don't know what he'll do."

With a lot of help from Clay and Roscoe, Anton managed to get on his horse. "We should be goin' after that bank robber," he grumbled. Clearly, he was getting weak from blood loss.

"We should be getting y'all to a doctor," Clay replied, and then he marched back to the saloon building. He came out toting the bank money, stuffed it into his saddle bag.

They were at the top of the last moraine when they saw two riders and the doctor's buggy coming across the flat prairie toward them. Clay spotted the cast on Toby's arm; the second rider was Chief Rowley, and Roscoe recognized Doc Hammond in the buggy.

"How'd y'all make it here so fast?" Clay asked when they met.

"We started out at dawn," Rowley explained. "I saw you and Helge leaving town last night... figured Helge was after the bounty and he knew something the sheriff's posse didn't."

Anton could barely keep himself in the saddle.

"He took a bullet in the leg," Roscoe said as he reached over to help steady the wounded bounty hunter.

Doc Hammond rushed to Anton. "Help me get him down," he ordered the others. "We'll put him in the back of my buggy." When Anton was in the buggy, Doc immediately went to work on his leg.

Clay took Chief Rowley aside. "Y'all will find a body in the fourth building on the left side of the street," he said. "His horse is between the next two buildings. I'm sorry... but I had to shoot him. He didn't leave me a choice."

"There should've been two," Rowley said.

"There was... but the second one got away."

"See which way he went?"

"No... I was inside the building... just saw him head for his horse."

"What'd he look like?"

Clay thought a moment. "Big guy... black hair, real mean-lookin' and he was wearing a blue shirt and a big black cowboy hat."

TWENTY-SEVEN

Toby and Doc Hammond had gone on ahead with Anton while the others returned to Newport to retrieve the dead bank robber. It was quite late that night when Clay, Roscoe and Chief Rowley made it back to Baraboo with the body slung over the saddle of his horse.

At the end of the long, tiring ride, Chief Rowley turned to Clay. "I've been watching how you handle yourself, Mr. Edwards. I think I could use someone like you on my police force."

"Are y'all offering me a job as a lawman?" Clay said.

"I'm prepared to pay you a good salary."

"Well, Chief, I'm flattered... but I don't think this is the place for me."

"Why not?"

"It's kind of personal, and besides... I've made

191

other plans."

"I see. And do your plans involve staying in Baraboo?"

"I don't think so, Chief... and thanks for the offer."

"Okay, but if you do change your mind, you know where to find me." The chief started to the undertaker's parlor with the body.

"Chief," Clay called out to him. He unbuckled the saddle bag and pulled out the bank loot. "Don't you want this?"

"Oh, yes... I'll get it back to them in the morning."

Clay and Roscoe got their horses back into the stable, and then they walked back to the Oak Street mercantile.

"There aren't any more trains back to the lake until morning," Roscoe said. "You might as well stay here tonight."

Clay didn't voice any objections; it had been an extremely long day. He was tired.

At the breakfast table the next morning, Mr. Connor was pleased that Roscoe and Clay had returned. "You must've concluded your business in Kilbourn quickly."

"Yes, sir."

"Actually, Pop," Roscoe said, "Clay shot another one of the bank robbers... and he got back the bank's money."

Jacob Connor nearly choked on a piece of bacon. "What? How did that happen?"

"Well, in all honesty, sir," Clay said. "That was the

business I had to attend to."

"How did you know where to find him?"

"Anton Helge... he invited me to accompany him... said he knew where they might've gone."

"You shoulda seen it, Pop! Anton got shot in the leg and so he couldn't do any more... so Clay 'n me cornered 'em in one of the old buildings at Newport... that's where Clay shot him dead."

"He didn't leave me any choice, sir... just want y'all to know that."

Even though Mr. Connor seemed a little disturbed about his son exposed to such danger, he couldn't help but congratulate Clay's actions. "Well, he was a thief and a murderer... I guess he got what he deserved."

"I'm glad y'all see it that way, sir."

Chief Rowley know about it yet?"

"Yeah, Pop. The chief and Doc Hammond followed us there, and a good thing, too... 'cause of Anton getting shot... and the chief brought back the body."

"I heard the bank is offering a sizeable reward."

"Yes," Clay replied. "But it was Anton who tracked 'em down... the reward will probably go to him."

Roscoe was back to work in the store; Clay was free to roam about for a while, as the next train to the lake wasn't due for a couple of hours. He decided his first stop should be at Theodore's Tailor Shop.

"NEW SUIT... NEW SUIT," the big colorful bird

squawked as he entered.

Theodore appeared from the back work room. "Aaaaah, Mr. Edwards, isn't it? So nice to see you again."

"NEW SUIT! NEW SUIT!"

"Napoleon!" Theodore scolded. "That's quite enough!" Then he turned to Clay again, eyeing his clothes that had recently become a bit tattered and frayed. "I see you are in need of some new garments."

"Yes, Theodore, I am... y'all can take my measurements today... but I would really like to talk to Ellie Mason, too."

Eleanor Mason flipped the curtain aside. "Did I hear someone mention my name?"

"Hello, Mrs. Mason," Clay greeted. "I have some good news for y'all... I found Marty."

"Where has he been this time?"

"He's in Kilbourn..."

"Kilbourn! What on earth is he doing there?"

"I... I... don't really know... but I'm sure he'll be home in a couple of days or so."

"That's a relief... I sure wish he'd tell me where he's going."

Theodore measured Clay for the new suit and assured him he could have it ready by the end of the week, derringer pocket in the sleeve and all.

"Good, Clay replied. "I shall stop in again on Friday."

As he left the tailor shop, Chief Rowley fell in step

with him.

"G' morning, Chief."

"G' morning, Mr. Edwards. Would you have a few moments to accompany me to the bank?"

"Well, I must get to the depot to catch the next train to the lake."

"This will only take a moment... it's very important."

Clay hadn't stopped thinking that Rowley would eventually figure out Marty's connection with the bank robbers. Rowley hadn't mentioned it yet, but now he was dragging Clay to the scene of the crime. "Okay... if it's absolutely necessary."

They walked to the next block and entered the bank; splintered recesses still showed in the walls where the bank robbers' bullets had struck, but business seemed to be back to normal. Rowley ushered Clay to a large office near the back of the lobby and knocked on the closed door.

"Come in," came a voice from inside.

Rowley opened the door; he and Clay stepped in.

"Well, Chief Rowley! I didn't expect you back so soon."

"I didn't have to go to the lake to find Mr. Edwards," the chief said. "He was right here in town."

The big, gray-haired man rose from behind his desk. He eyed Clay. "This must be Mr. Edwards."

"Clay Edwards." Clay offered his hand.

"I'm George Peterson, president of this bank." He shook Clay's hand firmly.

"Pleased to me y'all, Mr. Peterson."

"Chief Rowley tells me that you are responsible for recovering the bank's money... and gunning down those thieves."

Clay's face turned slightly red. "Well... yes... I guess I am. I'm sorry I had to kill them."

"You did what you had to do," Peterson said, re-assuring Clay with justification. He picked up a thick brown envelope from his desk. "On behalf of the Bank of Baraboo, I present you this reward... five thousand dollars... as promised." He held the envelope within Clay's reach.

"But we didn't catch the last one... he's still out there somewhere."

"I'm sure that other critter will get caught sooner or later. We got all our money back from the robbery... that's the important thing, Mr. Edwards."

Clay gracefully accepted the envelope. "There were others involved in this, y' know... I'll share it with them."

"You do as you see fit, Mr. Edwards."

"Thank you, sir."

With five thousand dollars cash in his coat pocket, Clay walked calmly down the street. He had abandoned the plan to get to the depot for now; he had more important things to do. He turned the corner and headed to Toby Atwood's house.

Mrs. Atwood opened the front door. A look of disgust covered her face. "How dare you come 'round here... after gettin' Toby almost kilt?"

"I'm sorry, Ma'am... but I think y'all should be very proud of your son's bravery. He saved Anton's life."

Toby came to the door. His cast wasn't white anymore, stained and smudged with dust and dirt. "Hi, Clay."

"Hi, Toby. I have something for y'all and your mother."

"What?" Toby asked curiously.

"Hold out your hand." Clay counted out two thousand dollars into Toby's upturned palm. "There. That's your share of the reward money." No other explanation was necessary.

Toby stared in disbelief.

Awestruck, Mrs. Atwood couldn't say another word.

Clay closed Toby's fingers around the cash. "Don't let the wind blow it away."

Toby finally regained his composure. "See, Ma? I told you Clay was a good person. And didn't I tell you that I'd find a way to get us some money." He turned to Clay with tears welling up in his eyes. "Thank you. I don't know what to say."

"Won't you come in?" Mrs. Atwood said. She was smiling now. "I just made a pitcher of cold lemonade."

"Thank you, Ma'am... but I really must be going. I have to catch a train."

He left Toby and his stammering mother on the front porch. Now they could survive nicely until Toby's arm healed and he could get back to work.

A pair of crutches leaned against one arm of a

big wicker chair where Anton sat on the front porch of his shabby little house, a yellow tabby cat curled up in his lap. His right leg was wrapped in white bandages, propped up on a stool. He shaded his eyes with one hand when he saw Clay coming across the tiny yard.

"Hello, Anton. How's the leg?"

"Mornin' Clay. Doc says I won't lose it... but it came close."

"I didn't know where to find y'all, so I asked Chief Rowley. Hope y'all don't mind."

"I hope you don't mind that I don't get up to shake your hand."

"Of course not. Does it hurt?"

"Only when I move."

"Well, I came over to see how y'all are... and to give y'all this." Clay pulled one thousand dollars from his coat pocket and handed it to Anton.

"What's this?"

"Your share of the reward."

"But you did all the dirty work. I didn't—"

"I want y'all to have it," Clay insisted. "Y'all gotta eat."

"But you 'n Roscoe should—"

"There's enough for all of us."

"And what 'bout that kid... Toby?"

"He got his share, too."

"Okay... good... 'cause if it wasn't for him, I might not be here."

The bell jangled as Clay entered the Mercantile.

Out of habit, Roscoe turned to see the arriving customer. Clay always warranted his immediate attention.

"I thought you were going back to the lake on the next train."

"Well, something came up. Can y'all get away for just a minute? I need to talk to y'all in private."

"Sure. I'll tell Pop." He zigzagged across the room among several customers, whispered something to his father, and then motioned to Clay to join him at the rear of the store. They slipped out through the back room and into the alley.

"Why all the secrecy?" Roscoe asked.

"I wanted this to be just between us. Hold out your hand."

TWENTY-EIGHT

I t had been nearly a week since they buried Simon. The pleasant May weather helped ease the sorrow, but his tragic loss was still painful. To add to the grief, now, once again, the Silver Spring Players were going their separate ways without having performed a single show together in Wisconsin. Claudia and Vivian were on their way to Chicago; Clyde and Charlotte were headed to San Francisco; Victor was returning to St. Louis and Henry to New Orleans. Christian and Clay saw them all off at the Devil's Lake Depot.

Clay returned to the lake Friday afternoon wearing the new Theodore-tailored suit. He and Christian sat at the Chateau overlooking the water, sipping ale and not discussing much of anything that had to do with either of their plans. Christian had been sulking for many days; Clay knew it was because of the theater building slipping out of his reach; he had wanted it more than anything, but now he, too, would have to plan a new strategy.

"Where do you suppose Marty disappeared to?" Christian asked.

It occurred to Clay that Marty's disappearance was part of Christian's low spirits. "I am quite confident that he's okay... that he'll just show up... like everybody says he will." Even though he had told Christian about the reward money and his harrowing experience with the third bank robber, he couldn't tell the whole story about what had happened at Newport; the last thing Christian needed was to form some negative feelings toward Marty. Marty could still be useful to Christian, and for Marty's sake, he hoped Christian would get him away from Baraboo.

Nor did he tell Christian that he had seen Marty in town earlier that day when he picked up his new suit at the tailor shop, or that he had invited Marty and Roscoe to join them for supper at the hotel.

They had just settled down at their supper table in the Cliff House dining room when two familiar faces appeared beside them. Christian's lower jaw practically bounced off the tablecloth.

Marty Mason was wearing his stunning new burgundy suit from Theodore's Tailor Shop. Roscoe Connor looked more like a gentleman gambler every day in his classy black three-piece, shiny boots and black hat.

"Mind if we join you?" Roscoe asked.

Clay motioned to the two empty chairs; his eyes fired a couple of warning shots in Marty's direction.

Christian beamed a grin. "I'm glad you're here," he said. "But where have you been?"

Marty glanced toward Clay for only a moment, and then fixed his eyes on Christian. "I... I... ran into a little difficulty last week... and I... I... couldn't make it to the lake. But I'll tell you about that another time."

"Y' see, Christian?" Clay said. "Told y'all he'd show up."

Just as Clay had instructed, Marty acted as if he were unaware of the past week's events. "I'm terribly sorry for not making it to the rehearsals..."

"Everything's different now," Christian said, a little sorrow tainting his words. Then he went on to explain to Marty about Simon's death, and about the rest of the Players leaving.

In reality, Marty knew about Simon, but he didn't know about the total breakup of the troupe. He stared questioningly at Christian, and then at Clay. "So... what do we do now?"

Clay gazed a long moment into Christian's eyes. Christian was a dear friend, and he meant a lot to Clay. But Clay had different desires now, and Christian was already aware that continuing in show business wasn't among them.

"My acting career is over," Clay told Marty.

"But... but... what will you do?"

"I'm going to London."

"London!"

"And from there, prob'ly Madrid... maybe Morocco. It's time for me to see the world. And Connor is going to see it with me."

Roscoe Connor grinned.

Marty stared at each one, bewildered. Then he turned his gaze to Christian.

"And I'm going to New York," Christian said. "To perform in the theaters there. How 'bout it, Mason? I could use a good piano man."

ABOUT THE AUTHOR

J.L. Fredrick lived his youth in rural Western Wisconsin, a modest but comfortable life not far from the Mississippi River. His father was a farmer, and his mother, an elementary school teacher. He attended a one-room country school for his first seven years of education.

Wisconsin has been home all his life, with exception of a few years in Minnesota and Florida. After college in La Crosse, Wisconsin and a stint with Uncle Sam during the Viet Nam era, the next few years were unsettled as he explored and experimented with life's options. He entered into the transportation industry in 1975 where he remained until retirement in 2012. He is a long-time member of the Wisconsin State Historical Society.

Since 2001 he has fourteen published novels to his credit, and two non-fiction history volumes, *Rivers, Roads, & Rails*, and *Ghostville*. He was a featured author during Grand Excursion 2004.

J.L. Fredrick currently resides at Poynette, Wisconsin.